DOVER · THRIFT · EDITIONS

The Oil Jar
and Other Stories

LUIGI PIRANDELLO

TRANSLATED BY STANLEY APPELBAUM

DOVER PUBLICATIONS, INC.
New York

CONTENTS

NOTE

The short stories of Luigi Pirandello (1867–1936) are brief, dynamic and full of tragic absurdity. The secret world of the individual personality, and the inevitable deceptions (and self-deceptions) that keep these personalities sane—or mad—form the main preoccupations of Pirandello's art, which also includes his poetry, novels and, most famously, his plays. Pirandello was awarded the Nobel Prize for Literature in 1934. The translations herein are based on the texts of the very first publications of the stories.

Bibliographical Note

This Dover edition, first published in 1995, reprints the complete English translations from the volume *Eleven Short Stories/Undici Novelle: A Dual-Language Book* (author: Pirandello), as published by Dover in 1994; the translations were newly prepared for that volume.

Library of Congress Cataloging-in-Publication Data

Pirandello, Luigi, 1867–1936.
    [Short stories. English. Selections]
    The oil jar and other stories / Luigi Pirandello ; translated by Stanley Appelbaum.
        p.   cm. — (Dover thrift editions)
    Contents : Little hut — Citrons from Sicily — With other eyes — A voice — The fly — The oil jar — It's not to be taken seriously — Think it over, Giacomino! — A character's tragedy — A prancing horse — Mrs. Frola and Mr. Ponza, her son-in-law.
    ISBN 0-486-28459-X (pbk.)
    1. Pirandello, Luigi, 1867–1936—Translations into English.   I. Appelbaum, Stanley.   II. Title.   III. Series.
PQ4835.I7A225 1995
853'.912—dc20
                                                                                94-41570
                                                                                CIP

Manufactured in the United States of America
Dover Publications, Inc., 31 East 2nd Street, Mineola, N.Y. 11501

LITTLE HUT

SICILIAN SKETCH.

A dawn like none ever seen.

A little girl came out of the small dark hut, with her hair tousled on her forehead and with a faded red kerchief on her head.

While she buttoned up her plain little dress, she was yawning, still confusedly half-asleep, and she was gazing: gazing into the distance, with her eyes wide open as if she saw nothing.

Far away, far away, a long streak of flaming red was strangely interwoven with the emerald green of the trees, which extended a great distance until disappearing from sight a long way off.

The entire sky was spattered with little clouds of a flaming saffron yellow.

The girl was walking inattentively, and there! . . . as a small hill that rose on the right was gradually lost to her view, the immensity of the waters of the sea was displayed before her eyes.

The girl seemed impressed, moved in the face of that scene, and stopped to look at the small boats that were skimming on the waves, tinged a pale yellow.

All was silence.—The gentle little night breeze was still blowing, creating trembling ripples on the sea, and slowly, slowly a pleasing smell of earth arose.

Shortly afterward the girl turned—wandered in that weak morning light and, when she reached the top of the rocky bank, sat down.

She absentmindedly viewed the green valley that smiled to her from below, and she had begun to hum a charming little song.

But all at once, as if struck by an idea, she stopped singing and, in the loudest tone she could muster, cried:

"'Uncle' Jeli! Oh, 'Uncle' Je . . . "[1]

And a coarse voice answered from the valley:

"Eh . . . "

"Climb up . . . because the boss wants you! . . . "

*

---

[1] "Uncle" and "aunt" were respectful terms of address in rural speech, for people older than the speaker but of the same social class.

Meanwhile the girl was returning toward the little hut, her head lowered.—Jeli had climbed up, still sleepy, with his jacket on his left shoulder and his pipe in his mouth—a pipe that he always allowed to sleep between his teeth.

As soon as he had come in, he greeted Papa Camillo, while Màlia, the steward's older daughter, looked him in the face with two eyes like arrows that could pierce a boulder.

Jeli responded to her look.

Papa Camillo was a little stump of a man, fat as a wine cask.

Màlia, on the other hand, had the face of one of Paolo Veronese's noblewomen, and in her eyes the blessed simplicity of her heart could be clearly read.

"Listen, Jeli," said Papa Camillo, "prepare some fruit because tomorrow the master and his family are coming from town.—Good ones, right? . . . otherwise . . . I swear to God! . . . "

"Oh! Always the same story," replied Jeli, "and you should know better than to say things like that . . . and to me of all people! . . . "

"Meanwhile," continued Papa Camillo and, taking him by the arm, led him out of the hut, "meanwhile . . . if you ever again take it into your head to . . . Enough! You understand me . . . "

Jeli seemed thunderstruck.

Papa Camillo went down through the valley.

The situation couldn't be better, and the young man dashed over to the little hut.

"We're lost!" said Màlia.

"Silly!" said Jeli. "If I don't succeed by fair means . . . "

"Oh! Jeli, Jeli, what do you mean?"

"What, you don't understand me? We'll run away."

"Run away?" said the girl, surprised.

"Or else . . . ," Jeli added, and he put his gleaming sickle around his neck . . .

"My God!" exclaimed Màlia, as if a shudder ran all through her body.

"This evening, you hear? At seven o'clock!" said Jeli, and vanished.

The girl uttered a cry.

It was becoming dark.

The arranged time was getting close and Màlia, extremely pale, with lips like two small petals of a dried rose, was sitting in front of the door.

She was looking at the green plain that was being submerged in darkness—and when, far off, the village bell rang the Angelus, she too prayed.

And that solemn silence was like a divine prayer of Nature!

After a long wait Jeli came. This time he had left behind his pipe, and was a little flushed and very determined.

"So early?" said Màlia, trembling.

"Fifteen minutes sooner, fifteen minutes later, it's all time gained," answered Jeli.

"But . . ."

"Damn it all! I think it's time to put aside all these 'buts' . . . Darling, don't you know what we're undertaking? . . . "

"I do know! I know it very well . . . ," Màlia hurriedly replied, unable to adjust to that rash determination.

Meanwhile a distant whistle informed Jeli that their conveyance was ready.

"Come on!" he said. "Be brave, my little Màlia! It's happiness that's calling for us . . . "

Màlia uttered a cry—Jeli took her by the arm, and off they ran . . .

As he set foot inside the farm wagon, he shouted: "As fast as you can!"

The two young people embraced and kissed freely for the first time.

At nine o'clock Papa Camillo returned from the valley and gave a loud whistle.

The little girl came hurriedly and before she arrived:

"Where is Jeli?" he asked her. "Have you seen Jeli?"

"Boss! . . . Boss! . . . " she replied in a breathless, stifled voice.

"What are you trying to tell me? Helpless simpleton!" roared Papa Camillo.

"Jeli . . . ran away . . . with Màlia . . . "

" . . . "

And a hoarse, . . . wild sound escaped Papa Camillo's throat.

He ran . . . flew to the hut: he took the carbine and fired into the air. The girl was watching, stunned.

That man's mad rage was a strange sight. A frenetic laugh burst from his lips and was lost in a choked rattle.—He no longer knew what he was doing . . . And, beside himself, he set fire to the little hut as if to destroy everything that spoke to him of his daughter.—Then, gun in hand, he raced furiously off down the path, where he perhaps hoped to find the lovers.

In the mournful evening those tongues of flame rose bloodred into the sky.

The little hut, blackened, was pouring out smoke, pouring smoke and crackling, as if with its slow snapping and popping it wanted to greet the little girl, who, pale, horrified, was watching it with fixed gaze.

All her thoughts seemed to be following the column of smoke that was rising from her humble dwelling . . .

The little hut, blackened, was pouring out smoke, pouring smoke and crackling, and the little girl stood there in silence, resting her gaze on the gloomy ashes.

Palermo '83

CITRONS FROM SICILY

"Is Teresina here?"

The servant—still in his shirt sleeves, but with his neck already squeezed into an extremely high collar and with his sparse hair carefully dressed and arranged on his cranium—raised his thick, joined eyebrows, which resembled a displaced mustache that had been shaved off his lips and pasted up there so he wouldn't lose it, and examined from head to foot the young man standing in front of him on the staircase landing: a rustic from the look of him, with the collar of his rough overcoat raised up to his ears and his hands—purple, numbed with cold—holding a dirty little sack on one side and a small old suitcase on the other, as a counterweight.

"Who is Teresina?"

The young man first shook his head to get rid of a little water drop on the tip of his nose, then replied:

"Teresina, the singer."

"Ah!" exclaimed the servant with a smile of ironic amazement: "That's her name, just plain Teresina? And who are you?"[1]

"Is she here or isn't she?" asked the young man, knitting his brows and sniffling. "Tell her that Micuccio is here, and let me in."

"But there's no one here," continued the servant with his smile congealed on his lips. "Madame Sina Marnis is still at the theater and . . ."

"Aunt Marta, too?" Micuccio interrupted him.

"Ah, you're a relative, sir? In that case, step right in, step right in . . . No one's at home. She's at the theater, too, your aunt. They won't be back before one. This is the benefit night[2] of your . . . what is she to you, the lady? Your cousin, perhaps?"

Micuccio stood there embarrassed for a moment.

---

[1] The night, contractually set aside, on which a member of a dramatic or operatic troupe would perform his or her specialties and share in the box-office take.

Micuccio stood there embarrassed for a moment.

"I'm not a relative . . . I'm Micuccio Bonavino, she knows . . . I've come on purpose from our hometown."

Upon receiving this reply, the servant deemed it suitable above all else to take back the polite *lei* form of address and go back to the ordinary *voi*; he led Micuccio into a small unlighted room near the kitchen, where someone was snoring noisily, and said to him:

"Sit here. I'll go and get a lamp."

Micuccio first looked in the direction from which the snoring was coming, but couldn't make out anything; then he looked into the kitchen, where the cook, aided by a scullery boy, was preparing a supper. The mingled aromas of the dishes being prepared over-powered him; their effect on him was like a heady intoxication; he had hardly eaten a thing since that morning; he had traveled from Reggio di Calabria: a night and a full day on the train.

The servant brought the lamp, and the person who was snoring in the room, behind a curtain hung from a cord between two walls, muttered sleepily:

"Who is it?"

"Hey, Dorina, get up!" the servant called. "Look, Mr. Bonvicino is here . . ."

"Bonavino," Micuccio corrected him, as he blew on his fingers.

"Bonavino, Bonavino . . . an acquaintance of the mistress. You really sleep soundly: they ring at the door and you don't hear it . . . I have to set the table; I can't do everything myself, under-stand—keep an eye on the cook, who doesn't know the ropes; watch for people who come to call . . ."

A big, loud yawn from the maid, prolonged while she stretched and ending in a whinny caused by a sudden shiver, was her reply to the complaint of the manservant, who walked away exclaiming:

"All right!"

Micuccio smiled and watched him depart across another room in semidarkness until he reached the vast, well-lit salon at the far end, where the splendid supper table towered; he kept on gazing in amazement until the snoring made him turn once more and look at the curtain.

The servant, with his napkin under his arm, passed back and forth, muttering now about Dorina, who went on sleeping, now about the cook, who was most likely a new man, called in for that evening's event, and who was annoying him by constantly asking for explanations. Micuccio, to avoid annoying him further, deemed it prudent to repress all the questions that he thought of asking him. He really ought to have told him or given him to understand that he was Teresina's fiancé, but he didn't want to, though he himself didn't know why, unless perhaps it was because the servant would then have had to treat him, Micuccio, as his master, and he, seeing him so jaunty and elegant, although still without his tailcoat, couldn't manage to overcome the embarrassment he felt at the very thought of it. At a certain point, however, seeing him pass by again, he couldn't refrain from asking him:

"Excuse me . . . whose house is this?"

"Ours, as long as we're in it," the servant answered hurriedly.

And Micuccio sat there shaking his head.

By heaven, so it was true! Opportunity seized by the forelock. Good business. That servant who resembled a great nobleman, the cook and the scullery boy, that Dorina snoring over there: all servants at Teresina's beck and call . . . Who would ever have thought so?

In his mind he saw once again the dreary garret, way down in Messina, where Teresa used to live with her mother . . . Five years earlier, in that faraway garret, if it hadn't been for him, mother and daughter would have died of hunger. And *he, he* had discovered that treasure in Teresa's throat! She was always singing, then, like a sparrow on the rooftops, unaware of her own treasure: she would sing to annoy, she would sing to keep from thinking of her poverty, which he would try to alleviate as best he could, in spite of the war his parents waged with him at home, his mother especially. But could he abandon Teresina in those circumstances, after her father's death?—abandon her because she had nothing, while he, for better or worse, did have a modest employment, as flute player in the local orchestra? Fine reasoning!—and what about his heart?

Ah, it had been a true inspiration from heaven, a prompting of fortune, when he had paid attention to that voice of hers, when no one was giving it heed, on that very beautiful April day, near the garret window that framed the vivid blue of the sky. Teresina was singing softly an impassioned Sicilian arietta, the tender words of which Micuccio still remembered. Teresina was sad, that day, over the recent death of her father and over his family's stubborn opposition; and he too—he recalled—was sad, so much so that tears had come to his eyes when he heard her sing. And yet he had heard that arietta many other times; but sung that way, never. He had been so struck by it that the following day, without informing her or her mother, he had brought with him his friend, the orchestra conductor, up to the garret. And in that way the first singing lessons had begun; and for two years running he had spent almost all of his small salary on her; he had rented a piano for her, had purchased her sheet music and had also given the teacher some friendly remuneration. Beautiful faraway days! Teresa burned intensely with the desire to take flight, to hurl herself into the future that her teacher promised her would be a brilliant one; and, in the meantime, what impassioned caresses for him to prove to him all her gratitude, and what dreams of happiness together!

Aunt Marta, on the other hand, would shake her head bitterly: she had seen so many ups and downs in her life, poor old lady, that by now she had no more trust left in the future; she feared for her daughter and didn't want her even to think about the possibility of escaping that poverty to which they were resigned; and, besides, she knew, she knew how much the madness of that dangerous dream was costing him.

But neither he nor Teresina would listen to her, and she protested in vain when a young composer, having heard Teresina at a concert, declared that it would be a real crime not to give her better teachers and thorough artistic instruction: in Naples, it was essential to send her to the Naples conservatory, cost what it might.

And then he, Micuccio, breaking off with his parents altogether, had sold a little farm of his that had been bequeathed to him by his uncle the priest, and in that way Teresina had gone to Naples to perfect her studies.

He hadn't seen her again since then; but he had received her letters from the conservatory and afterwards those of Aunt Marta, when Teresina was already launched on her artistic life, eagerly sought by the major theaters after her sensational debut at the San Carlo. At the foot of those shaky and hesitant letters, which the poor old lady scratched onto the paper as best she could, there were always a few words from *her,* from Teresina, who never had time to write: "Dear Micuccio, I go along with everything Mother is telling you. Stay healthy and keep caring for me." They had agreed that he would leave her five or six years' time to pursue her career without impediment: they were both young and could wait.

And in the five years that had already elapsed, he had always shown those letters to anyone who wanted to see them, to combat the slanderous remarks his family would hurl at Teresina and her mother. Then he had fallen sick; he had been on the point of dying; and on that occasion, without his knowledge, Aunt Marta and Teresina had sent to his address a large sum of money; part had been spent during his illness, but the rest he had violently torn out of his family's hands and now, precisely, he was coming to return it to Teresina. Because money—no! He didn't want any. Not because it seemed like a handout, seeing that he had already spent so much on her; but . . . no! He himself was unable to say why, and now more than ever, there, in that house . . . money, no! Just as he had waited all those years, he could wait some more . . . Because if Teresina actually had money to spare, it was a sign that the future was now open to her, and therefore it was time for the old promise to be kept, in spite of anyone who refused to believe it.

Micuccio stood up with his brows knitted, as if to reassure himself about that conclusion; once again he blew on his ice-cold hands and stamped on the floor.

"Cold?" the servant said to him passing by. "It won't be long now. Come here into the kitchen. You'll be more comfortable."

Micuccio didn't want to follow the advice of the servant, who confused and irritated him with that lordly air. He sat down again and resumed thinking in dismay. Shortly afterward a loud ring roused him.

"Dorina, the mistress!" screamed the servant, hurriedly slipping on his tailcoat as he ran to open the door; but seeing that Micuccio was about to follow him, he stopped short and issued an order:

"You stay there; let me notify her first."

"Ohi, ohi, ohi . . . ," lamented a sleepy voice behind the curtain; and after a moment there appeared a large, stocky, carelessly dressed woman who trailed one leg on the ground and was still unable to keep her eyes open; she had a woolen shawl pulled up over her nose and her hair was dyed gold.

Micuccio kept looking at her foolishly. She too, in her surprise, opened her eyes wide when confronted by the outsider.

"The mistress," Micuccio repeated.

Then Dorina suddenly returned to consciousness:

"Here I am, here I am . . . ," she said, taking off the shawl and flinging it behind the curtain, and exerting her whole heavy body to run toward the entrance.

The apparition of that dyed witch, and the order given by the servant, suddenly gave Micuccio, in his dejection, an anguished presentiment. He heard Aunt Marta's shrill voice:

"Over there, into the salon, into the salon, Dorina!"

And the servant and Dorina passed by him carrying magnificent baskets of flowers. He leaned his head forward so he could observe the illuminated room at the far end, and he saw a great number of gentlemen in tailcoats talking confusedly. His sight grew dim; his amazement and agitation were so great that he himself didn't realize that his eyes had filled with tears; he closed them, and he shut himself up completely in that darkness, as if to resist the torment that a long, ringing laugh was causing him. It was Teresina laughing like that, in the other room.

A muffled cry made him open his eyes again, and he saw before him—unrecognizable—Aunt Marta, with her hat on her head, poor thing! and laden down by a costly and splendid velvet mantilla.

"What! Micuccio . . . you here?"

"Aunt Marta . . . ," exclaimed Micuccio, almost frightened, pausing to examine her closely.

"Whatever for?" continued the old lady, who was upset. "Without letting us know? What happened? When did you get here? . . . Tonight of all nights . . . Oh, God, God . . ."

"I've come to . . . ," Micuccio stammered, not knowing what more to say.

"Wait!" Aunt Marta interrupted him. "What's to be done? What's to be done? See all those people, son? It's Teresina's celebration . . . her night . . . Wait, wait here for a bit . . ."

"If you," Micuccio attempted to say, as anxiety tightened his throat, "if you think I ought to go . . ."

"No, wait a bit, I say," the kind old lady hastened to reply, all embarrassed.

"But," Micuccio responded, "I have no idea where to go in this town . . . at this hour . . ."

Aunt Marta left him, signaling to him with one of her gloved hands to wait, and entered the salon, in which a moment later Micuccio thought an abyss had opened; silence had suddenly fallen there. Then he heard, clear and distinct, these words of Teresina:

"One moment, gentlemen."

Again his sight grew dim with the imminence of her appearance. But Teresina did not come, and the conversation resumed in the salon. Instead, after a few minutes, which seemed an eternity to him, Aunt Marta came back, without her hat, without her mantilla, without her gloves, and less embarrassed.

"Let's wait here for a while, would that be all right?" she said to him. "I'll stay with you . . . Now they're having supper . . . We'll remain here. Dorina will set this little table for us, and we'll have supper together, here; we'll reminisce about the good old days, all right? . . . I can't believe it's true that I'm here with you, son, here, here, all by ourselves . . . In that room, you understand, all those gentlemen . . . She, poor girl, can't avoid them . . . Her career, you get my meaning? Ah, what can you do! . . . Have you seen the newspapers? Big doings, son! As for me, I'm all at sea, all the time . . . I can't believe I can really be here with you, tonight."

And the kind old lady, who had gone on talking, instinctively, to keep Micuccio from having time to think, finally smiled and rubbed her hands together, looking at him compassionately.

Dorina came to set the table hastily, because there, in the salon, the meal had already begun.

"Will she come?" Micuccio asked gloomily, with a troubled voice. "I mean, at least to see her."

"Of course she'll come," the old lady immediately replied, making an effort to get out of her awkward situation. "Just as soon as she has a minute free: she's already told me so."

They looked at each other and smiled at each other, as if they had finally recognized each other. Despite the embarrassment and the excitement, their souls had found the way to greet each other with that smile. "You're Aunt Marta," Micuccio's eyes said. "And you're Micuccio, my dear, good son, still the same, poor boy!" said Aunt Marta's. But suddenly the kind old lady lowered her own eyes, so that Micuccio might not read anything else in them. Again she rubbed her hands together and said:

"Let's eat, all right?"

"I'm good and hungry!" exclaimed Micuccio, quite happy and reassured.

"Let's cross ourselves first: here, in front of you, I can do it," added the old lady in a mischievous manner, winking an eye, and she made the sign of the cross.

The manservant came, bringing their first course. Micuccio observed with close attention the way that Aunt Marta transferred her helping from the serving platter. But when his turn came, as he raised his hands, it occurred to him that they were dirty from the long trip; he blushed, he got confused, he raised his eyes to steal a glance at the servant, who, now the height of good manners, nodded slightly to him and smiled, as if inviting him to serve himself. Fortunately Aunt Marta helped him out of his predicament.

"Here, here, Micuccio, I'll serve you."

He could have kissed her out of gratitude! Once he received his helping, as soon as the servant had withdrawn, he too crossed himself hurriedly.

"Good boy!" Aunt Marta said to him.

And he felt carefree, contented, and started eating as he had never eaten in his life, no longer thinking about his hands or the servant.

Nevertheless, each and every time the latter, entering or leaving the salon, opened the glass double door, and a sort of wave of mingled words or some burst of laughter came from that direction, he turned around uneasily and then looked at the old lady's sorrowful, loving eyes, as if to read an explanation there. But what he read there instead was an urgent request to ask no more for the moment, to put off explanations till a later time. And again they both smiled at each other and resumed eating and talking about their far-off hometown, friends and acquaintances, concerning whom Aunt Marta asked him for news endlessly.

"Aren't you drinking?"

Micuccio put out his hand to take the bottle; but, just at that moment, the double door to the ballroom opened again; a rustle of silk, amid hurried steps: a flash, as if the little room had all at once been violently illuminated, in order to blind him.

"Teresina . . ."

And his voice died away on his lips, out of amazement. Ah, what a queen!

With face flushed, eyes bulging and mouth open, he stopped to gaze at her, dumbfounded. How could she ever . . . like that! Her bosom bare, her shoulders bare, her arms bare . . . all ablaze with jewels and rich fabrics . . . He didn't see her, he no longer saw her as a living, real person in front of him . . . What was she saying to him? . . . Not her voice, nor her eyes, nor her laugh: nothing, nothing of hers did he recognize any more in that dream apparition.

"How are things? Are you getting along all right now, Micuccio? Good, good . . . You were sick if I'm not mistaken . . . We'll get together again in a little while. In the meantime, you have Mother with you here . . . Is that a deal? . . ."

And Teresina ran off again into the salon, all a-rustle.

"You're not eating any more?" Aunt Marta asked timorously after a brief pause, to cut short Micuccio's silent astonishment.

He looked at her in bewilderment.

"Eat," the old lady insisted, showing him his plate.

Micuccio raised two fingers to his smoke-blackened, crumpled collar and tugged at it, trying to draw a deep breath.

"Eat?"

And several times he wiggled his fingers near his chin as if waving goodbye, to indicate: I don't feel like it any more, I can't. For another while he remained silent, dejected, absorbed in the vision he had just seen, then he murmured:

"How she's turned out . . ."

And he saw that Aunt Marta was shaking her head bitterly and that she too had stopped eating, as if in expectation.

"It's not even to be thought of . . . ," he then added, as if to himself, closing his eyes.

Now he saw, in that darkness of his, the gulf that had opened between the two of them. No, she—that woman—was no longer his Teresina. It was all over . . . for some time, for some time, and he, the fool, he, the imbecile, was realizing it only now. They had told him so back home, and he had stubbornly refused to believe it . . . And now, how would he look staying on in that house? If all those gentlemen, if even that servant had known that he, Micuccio Bonavino, had worn himself out coming such a distance, thirty-six hours by train, seriously believing he was still the fiancé of that queen, what laughs they would raise, those gentlemen and that servant and the cook and the scullery boy and Dorina! What laughs, if Teresina had dragged him into their presence, in the salon there, saying: "Look, this pauper, this flute player, says he wants to become my husband!" She, yes, she had promised him this; but how could she herself suppose at that time that one day she would become what she now was? And it was also true, yes, that he had opened that path for her and had given her the means to travel it; but, there! by this time she had come so very far, how could he, who had stayed where he was, always the same, playing the flute on Sundays in the town square, catch up to her any more? It wasn't even to be thought of! And, then, what were those few paltry cents spent on her back then, now that she had become a great lady? He was ashamed merely to think that someone might suspect that he, with his coming, wanted to assert some rights in exchange for those few miserable pennies . . .—But at that moment he remembered that he had in his pocket the money sent him by Teresina during his illness. He blushed: he felt a twinge of shame, and he plunged one hand into the breast pocket of his jacket, where his wallet was.

"I've come, Aunt Marta," he said hastily, "also to return to you this money you sent me. Is it meant as a payment? As repayment of a loan? What would that have to do with anything? I see that Teresina has become a . . . she looks like a queen to me! I see that . . . never mind! It's not even to be thought of any longer! But as for this money, no: I didn't deserve such treatment from her . . . Where does that come in? It's all over, and we won't talk about it any more . . . but money, no way! I'm only sorry that it's not all here . . ."

"What are you saying, son?" Aunt Marta tried to interrupt him, trembling, pained and with tears in her eyes.

Micuccio signaled to her to be silent.

"It wasn't I who spent it: my family spent it, during my illness, without my knowledge. But let's say it makes up for that trifle I spent back then . . . you remember? It doesn't matter . . . Let's think no more about it. Here is the difference. And I'm leaving."

"What! Like that, all of a sudden?" exclaimed Aunt Marta, trying to hold him back. "At least wait until I tell Teresina. Didn't you hear that she wanted to see you again? I'm going over to tell her . . ."

"No, it's no use," Micuccio replied, with determination. "Let her stay there with those gentlemen; it suits her there, she belongs there. I, poor fool . . . I got to see her; that was enough for me . . . No, now that I think of it, do go over there . . . you go there, too . . . Do you hear how they're laughing? I don't want the laugh to be on me . . . I'm leaving."

Aunt Marta interpreted that sudden determination of Micuccio's in the worst possible light: as an act of anger, a jealous reaction. By now it seemed to her, the poor woman, as if everybody—seeing her daughter—ought immediately to conceive the meanest of suspicions, that very one which caused her to weep inconsolably as, without a moment's rest, she bore the burden of her secret heartbreak amid the hubbub of that life of detestable luxury which ignominiously dishonored her old age.

"But I," the words escaped her, "by this time there's no way for me to stand guard over her, son . . ."

"Why?" asked Micuccio, suddenly reading in her eyes the suspicion he had not yet formulated; and his face turned dark.

The old lady became bewildered in her sorrow and hid her face in her trembling hands, but failed to check the onrush of the tears that now gushed forth.

"Yes, yes, go, son, go . . .," she said, strangled by sobs. "She's not for you any more, you're right . . . If the two of you had listened to me . . ."

"And so," Micuccio burst out, bending over her and violently pulling one hand away from her face. But so afflicted and wretched was the look with which she begged him for mercy, as she put a finger to her lips, that he restrained himself and added in a different tone of voice, making an effort to speak softly: "And so she, she . . . she is no longer worthy of me. Enough, enough, I'm leaving just the same . . . in fact, all the more, now . . . What a dumbbell, Aunt Marta: I hadn't understood! Don't cry . . . Anyway, what does it matter? Fate . . . fate . . ."

He took his little suitcase and little sack from under the table and was on his way out when he recalled that there, in the sack, were the beautiful citrons he had brought for Teresina from their hometown.

"Oh, look, Aunt Marta," he continued. He opened the top of the sack and, creating a barrier with one arm, he emptied that fresh, aromatic fruit onto the table. "And what if I started tossing all these citrons I brought for her at the heads of those honorable gentlemen?"

"For mercy's sake," the old lady groaned amid her tears, once more making a beseeching sign to him to be silent.

"No, of course I won't," added Micuccio, smiling sourly and putting the empty sack in his pocket. "I'm leaving them for you alone, Aunt Marta. And to think that I even paid duty on them . . . Enough. For you alone, mind me now. As for her, tell her 'Good luck!' from me."

He picked up the valise again and left. But on the stairs, a sense of anguished bewilderment overpowered him: alone, deserted, at night, in a big city he didn't know, far from his home; disappointed, dejected, put to shame. He made it to the street door, saw that there was a downpour of rain. He didn't have the courage to venture onto those unfamiliar streets in a rain like that. He went back in very quietly, walked back up one flight of stairs, then sat down on the first step and, leaning his elbows on his knees and his head on his hands, began to weep silently.

When the supper was finished, Sina Marnis made another appearance in the little room; but she found her mother alone crying, while back there the gentlemen were clamoring and laughing.

"He left?" she asked in surprise.

Aunt Marta nodded affirmatively, without looking at her. Sina stared into space, lost in thoughts, then sighed:

"Poor guy . . ."

"Look," her mother said to her, no longer stemming her tears with the tablecloth. "He had brought citrons for you . . ."

"Oh, what beauties!" exclaimed Sina, cheering up. She clutched one arm to her waist and with the other hand gathered up as many as she could carry.

"No, not in there!" her mother vigorously protested.

But Sina shrugged her bare shoulders and ran into the salon shouting:

"Citrons from Sicily! Citrons from Sicily!"

WITH OTHER EYES

Through the large window that opened onto the house's little hanging garden, the pure, fresh morning air made the pretty little room cheerful. An almond branch, which seemed to be all a-blossom with butterflies, projected toward the window; and, mingled with the hoarse, muffled gurgle of the small basin in the center of the garden, was heard the festive peal of faraway churchbells and the chirping of the swallows intoxicated with the air and the sunshine.

As she stepped away from the window, sighing, Anna noticed that her husband that morning had forgotten to rumple his bed, as he used to do each time, so that the servants couldn't tell that he hadn't slept in his room. She rested her elbows on the untouched bed, then stretched out on it with her whole torso, bending her pretty blonde head over the pillows and half-closing her eyes, as if to savor, in the freshness of the linens, the slumbers he was accustomed to enjoy there. A flock of swallows flashed headlong past the window, shrieking.

"You would have done better to sleep here . . . ," she murmured languidly after a moment, and got up again wearily.

Her husband was to set out that very evening, and Anna had come into his room to prepare for him the things he needed for the trip.

As she opened the wardrobe, she heard what seemed to be a squeak in the inner drawer and quickly drew back, startled. From a corner of the room she picked up a walking stick with a curved handle and, holding her dress tight against her legs, took the stick by the tip and, standing that way at a distance, tried to open the drawer with it. But as she pulled, instead of the drawer coming out, an insidious gleaming blade emerged smoothly from inside the stick. Anna, who hadn't expected this, felt an extreme repulsion and let the scabbard of the swordstick drop from her hand.

At that moment, a second squeak made her turn abruptly toward the window, uncertain whether the first one as well had come from some rapidly passing swallow.

With one foot she pushed aside the unsheathed weapon and

pulled out, between the two open doors of the wardrobe, the drawer full of her husband's old suits that he no longer wore. Out of sudden curiosity she began to rummage around in it and, as she was putting back a worn-out, faded jacket, she happened to feel, in the hem under the lining, a sort of small paper, which had slipped down there through the torn bottom of the breast pocket; she wanted to see what that paper was which had gone astray and been forgotten there who knows how many years ago; and so by accident Anna discovered the portrait of her husband's first wife.

At first she had a start and turned pale; she quickly ran a hand through her hair, which was shaken by a shudder and, with her vision blurred and her heart stopped, she ran to the window, where she remained in astonishment gazing at the unfamiliar image, almost with a feeling of panic.

The bulky hair style and the old-fashioned dress kept her from noticing at first the beauty of that face; but as soon as she was able to concentrate on the features, separating them from the attire, which now, after so many years, looked ludicrous, and to pay special attention to the eyes, she felt wounded by them and, together with her blood, a flush of hatred leaped from her heart to her brain; a hatred as if caused by posthumous jealousy; that hatred mingled with contempt which she had felt for that other woman when she fell in love with Vittore Brivio, eleven years after the marital tragedy that had at one blow destroyed his first household.

Anna had hated that woman, unable to comprehend how she had been capable of betraying the man whom she now worshiped, and in the second place, because her family had objected to her marriage with Brivio, as if *he* had been responsible for the disgrace and violent death of his unfaithful wife.—It was she, yes, it was she beyond a doubt! Vittore's first wife: the one who had killed herself!

She found the proof in the dedication written on the back of the portrait: "To my Vittore, his Almira—November 11, 1873."

Anna had very vague information about the dead woman: she knew only that Vittore, when the betrayal was discovered, had, with the impassivity of a judge, forced her to take her own life.

Now with satisfaction she recalled that terrible sentence issued by her husband, and was irritated by that "my" and "his" of the dedication, as if the other woman had wished to flaunt the closeness of the mutual ties that had bound her and Vittore, solely to spite her.

That first flare-up of hatred, ignited, like a will-o'-the-wisp, by a rivalry which by now existed only for her, was succeeded in Anna's mind by feminine curiosity: she desired to examine the features of that face, although she was partially restrained by the odd sorrow one feels at the sight of an object that belonged to a person who died tragically—a sorrow that was sharper now, but not unfamiliar to her, because it permeated her love for her husband, who had formerly belonged to that other woman.

Examining her face, Anna immediately noticed how entirely dissimilar it was to hers, and at the same time there arose in her heart the question of how the husband who had loved that woman, that girl, whom he must have found beautiful, could ever have later fallen in love with *her*, who was so different.

It seemed beautiful, even to her it seemed much more beautiful than hers—that face which, from the portrait, looked swarthy. There!—those lips had joined in a kiss with his lips; but why that sorrowful crease at the corners of the mouth? And why was the gaze in those intense eyes so sad? The entire face spoke of deep suffering; and Anna was moved and almost vexed by the humble and genuine kindness expressed by those features, and after that she felt a twinge of repulsion and disgust, when all at once she believed she had observed in the gaze of those eyes the same expression her own eyes had, whenever, thinking of her husband, she looked at herself in the mirror, in the morning, after arranging her hair.

She had barely enough time to thrust the portrait into her pocket: her husband appeared, fuming, on the threshold to the room.

"What have you been doing? The usual thing? Every time you come into this room to straighten up, you rearrange everything. . . ."

Then, seeing the unsheathed swordstick on the floor:

"Have you been fencing with the suits in the wardrobe?"

And he laughed that laugh of his which came only from the throat, as if someone had tickled him there; and, laughing in that fashion, he looked at his wife, as if asking *her* why he himself was laughing. As he looked, his eyelids constantly blinked with extreme rapidity against his sharp, black, restless little eyes.

Vittore Brivio treated his wife like a child capable of nothing but that ingenuous, exclusive and almost childish love with which he felt himself surrounded, frequently to his annoyance, and to which he had determined to pay attention only on due occasion, and even at those times displaying an indulgence partially mixed with light irony, as if he meant to say: "All right, have it your way! For a while I too will become a child along with you: this, too, must be done, but let's not waste too much time!"

Anna had let the old jacket in which she had found the portrait drop to her feet. He picked it up, piercing it with the point of the swordstick; then, through the garden window he called the young servant who also doubled as a coachman and was at that moment harnessing the horse to the cabriolet. As soon as the boy showed up, in his shirt sleeves, in the garden in front of the window, Brivio rudely threw the dangling jacket in his face, accompanying the handout with a: "Take it, it's yours."

"This way, you'll have less to brush," he added, turning toward his wife, "and to straighten up, I hope!"

And again, blinking, he uttered that stentorean laugh of his.

On other occasions her husband had traveled out of the city, and not merely for a few days, also leaving at night like this time; but Anna, still extremely shaken by the discovery of the portrait on that very day, felt a strange fear of being left alone and wept when she said goodbye to him.

Vittore Brivio, in a great rush from fear of being late and evidently preoccupied with his business, reacted ill-manneredly to those uncustomary tears of his wife.

"What! Why? Come on now, come on now, that's so childish!"

And he left in hot haste, without even saying goodbye.

Anna jumped at the sound of the door that he closed behind him with force; she remained in the little room with the lamp in her hand and felt her tears growing cold in her eyes. Then she roused herself and hurriedly withdrew to her room, intending to go to bed at once.

In the room, which was already prepared, the little night light was burning.

"Go to bed," Anna said to the maid who was waiting for her. "I'll take care of things myself. Good night."

She extinguished the lamp, but instead of putting it on the shelf, as she usually did, she put it on the night table, with the feeling—actually against her will—that she might need it later. She started to undress hastily, gazing fixedly at the floor in front of her. When her dress fell around her feet, it occurred to her that the portrait was there, and with acute vexation she felt herself being looked at and pitied by those sorrowful eyes, which had made such an impression on her. With determination she stooped down to pick up the dress from the carpet and, without folding it, she placed it on the armchair at the foot of the bed, as if the pocket that hid the portrait and the tangle of the fabric should and could prevent her from reconstructing the image of that dead woman.

As soon as she lay down, she closed her eyes and forced herself to follow her husband mentally along the road leading to the railroad station. She forced this upon herself as a spiteful rebellion against the feeling that had kept her alert all day long observing and studying her husband. She knew where that feeling had come from and she wanted to get rid of it.

In this effort of her will, which caused her an acute nervous agitation, she pictured to herself with an extraordinary second sight the long road, deserted at night, illuminated by the streetlamps projecting their wavering light onto the pavement, which seemed to palpitate because of it; at the foot of every lamp, a circle of shadow; the shops, all closed; and there was the carriage in which Vittore was riding: as if she had been lying in wait for it, she started following it all the way to the station: she saw the gloomy train beneath the glass shed; a great many people milling about in that vast, smoky, poorly lit, mournfully echoing interior: now the train was pulling out; and, as if she were really watching it move away and disappear into the darkness, she suddenly came back to herself, opened her eyes in the silent room and felt an anguished feeling of emptiness, as if something were missing inside her. She then felt confusedly, in a flash, becoming bewildered, that for three years perhaps, from the moment in which she had left her parents' home, she had been in that void of which she was only now becoming conscious. She had been unaware of it before, because she had filled that void with herself alone, with her love; she was becoming aware of it now, because all day long she had, as it were, suspended her love in order to look and to observe.

"He didn't even say goodbye to me," she thought; and she started to cry again, as if that thought were the definite reason for her tears.

She sat up in bed: but she suddenly held back the hand she had stretched out, while sitting up, to get her handkerchief from her dress. No, it was no longer any use to forbid herself to take another look at that portrait, to reexamine it! She took it. She put the light back on.

How differently she had pictured that woman! Now, contemplating her real likeness, she felt remorse for the feelings that the imaginary woman had aroused in her. She had pictured a woman rather fat and ruddy, with flashing, smiling eyes, always ready to laugh, enjoying common amusements . . . And instead, now, there she was: a young woman whose cleancut features expressed a profound, sorrowful soul; whose eyes expressed a sort of all-absorbing silence; yes, different from herself, but not in that earlier vulgar sense: just the opposite; no, that mouth looked as if it had never smiled, whereas her own had laughed so often and so gaily; and surely, if that face was swarthy (as it seemed to be from the portrait), it had a less smiling air than her own blonde and rosy face.

Why, why so sad?

A hateful thought flashed across her mind, and all at once with violent repulsion she tore her eyes away from that woman's picture, suddenly discovering in it a snare threatening not only to her peace of mind, to her love, which, as it was, had received more than one wound that day, but also to her proud dignity as an honest woman who had never allowed herself even the remotest thought hostile to her husband.

That woman had had a lover! And perhaps it was because of him she was so sad, because of that adulterous love, and not because of her husband!

She tossed the portrait onto the bedside table and put out the light again, hoping to fall asleep this time without thinking any more about that woman, with whom she could have nothing in common. But, closing her eyes, she suddenly saw, in spite of herself, the dead woman's eyes, and sought in vain to dispel that sight.

"Not because of him, not because of him!" she then murmured with frenzied persistence, as if by insulting her she hoped to be rid of her.

And she made an effort to recall everything she knew about that other man, the lover, as if compelling the gaze and the sadness of those eyes to look no longer at her but at the former lover, whom she knew only by name: Arturo Valli. She knew that he had married a few years later as if to prove his innocence of the blame that Vittore wanted to ascribe to him, that he had vigorously declined Vittore's challenge to a duel, protesting that he would never fight with a mad killer. After this refusal, Vittore had threatened to kill him wherever he came across him, even in church; and then he had left the town with his wife, returning later as soon as Vittore, remarried, had departed.

But from the sadness of those events which she now brought back to mind, from Valli's cowardice and, after so many years, from the way the first wife had been completely consigned to oblivion by her husband, who had been able to resume his life and remarry as if nothing had happened, from the joy that she herself had felt upon becoming Vittore's wife, from those three years she had spent together with him with never a thought about that other woman, unexpectedly a cause of pity for her spontaneously forced itself upon Anna; she saw her image again vividly and it seemed to her that with those eyes, intense from so much suffering, that woman was saying to her:

"But I'm the only one that died as a result! All of you are still living!"

She saw, she felt, that she was alone in the house: she got frightened. Yes, *she* was living; but for three years, since her wedding day, she hadn't seen her parents or sister, not even once. She who adored them, a dutiful daughter, a trusting sister, had had the courage to oppose their wishes out of love for her husband; for his sake, when he was rejected by his own family, she had fallen seriously ill, and would no doubt have died if the doctors hadn't induced her father to accede to her desire. And her father had yielded, but without giving his consent; in fact, he swore that after that wedding she would no longer exist for him or for that household. Besides the difference in age, the husband being eighteen years older than the wife, a more serious obstacle for the father had been Brivio's financial position, which was subject to rapid ups and downs because of the risky undertakings on which this most enterprising and extraordinarily active man was accustomed to embark with foolhardy confidence in himself and his luck.

In three years of marriage Anna, surrounded by comforts, had been able to consider as unjust, or dictated by hostile prejudice, her father's prudent misgivings as to the financial means of her husband, in whom, moreover, in her ignorance, she placed as much confidence as he had in himself; then, as for the difference in their ages, up to then there had been no manifest cause of disappointment for her or surprise for others, because Brivio's advanced years produced in him not the slightest impairment to his small, highly animated and robust body and even less to his mind, which was endowed with tireless energy and restless eagerness.

It was something totally different that Anna, now for the first time, looking into her life (without even realizing it) with the eyes of that dead woman depicted there in the portrait on the bedside table, found to complain of in her husband. Yes, it was true: she had felt hurt at other times by his almost disdainful indifference; but never so much as on that day; and now for the first time she felt so frighteningly alone, separated from her family, who at that moment seemed to her to have abandoned her there, as if, upon marrying Brivio, she already had something in common with that dead woman and was no longer worthy of anyone else's company. And her husband, who ought to have consoled her, it seemed that even her husband was unwilling to give her any credit for the sacrifice of her daughterly and sisterly love that she had offered him, just as if it had cost her nothing, as if he had had a right to that sacrifice and therefore had no obligation now to make it up to her. Yes, he had a right, but it was because she had fallen so totally in love with him at that time; therefore he now had an obligation to repay her. And instead . . .

"It's always been like that!" Anna thought she heard the sorrowful lips of the dead woman sigh to her.

She lit the lamp again and once more, contemplating the picture, she was struck by the expression of those eyes. So then, it was true, she too had suffered on his account? She too, she too, realizing she wasn't loved, had felt that frightening emptiness?

"Yes? Yes?" Anna, choking with tears, asked the picture.

And it then seemed to her that those kindly eyes, intense with passion and heartbreak, were pitying her in their turn, were condoling with her over that abandonment, that unrequited sacrifice, that love which remained locked up in her breast like a treasure in a casket to which he had the keys but would never use them, like a miser.

A VOICE

A few days before she died, the Marchesa Borghi, more from a qualm of conscience than for any other reason, had decided to consult even Dr. Giunio Falci regarding her son Silvio, who had been blind for about a year. She had had him examined at home by the most famous oculists in Italy and abroad, and all of them had told her that he was suffering from incurable glaucoma.

Dr. Giunio Falci had recently gained the position of director of the eye clinic by competitive examination; but, whether it was due to his weary and always absentminded manner, or whether it was due to his ungraceful appearance—that completely lax and listless way he had of walking, with his big, prematurely bald, uncovered head thrown back, his long, thin nose in the air, like a sail on his bony, emaciated little face with its short, sparse, rough beard, already somewhat gray, parted on his chin—he was liked so little by people in general that many even went so far as to deny him any medical skill. He was aware of this and seemed to enjoy the situation. He became more absentminded daily and no longer shook himself out of his weary stupefaction except to pose curious, penetrating questions that chilled and disconcerted the listener. He had gradually formed a concept of life so devoid of all those friendly and almost necessary hypocrisies, those spontaneous, inevitable illusions composed and created by each of us without our volition, through an instinctive need—for social decency, one might say—that his company had now become intolerable.

At the invitation of the Marchesa Borghi, he had gone one morning to the airy, solitary new street, lined with villas, at the far end of Castle Meadows, across Margherita Bridge; he had made a long, careful examination of the young man's eyes, without paying attention—at least seemingly—to all that the Marchesa was telling him in the meantime about the ailment, the diagnoses of the other doctors and the various cures that had been tried. Glaucoma? No. He did not think he had found in those eyes the characteristic signs of that complaint, the bluish or greenish color of the opacity, etc., etc.; instead, he had decided that what he had before him was a rare and strange manifestation of that disease commonly known as cataract. But he had not wished to reveal his doubt to the mother all at once, in order to keep her from suddenly cherishing even the slenderest hope; besides, he himself did not feel entirely sure of the matter. Instead, disguising the very keen interest awakened in him by that strange case, he had declared his wish to call on the patient again in a few days.

And he had in fact returned; but, oddly, on that new, always deserted street at the far end of Castle Meadows where the Marchesa Borghi's villa was located, he had found a crowd of curious onlookers in front of the open gate of the villa. The Marchesa Borghi had died suddenly during the night.

What should he do? Turn back? Then it had occurred to him that, if on his first call he had expressed his opinion that, from his point of view, the young man's ailment was not really glaucoma, perhaps that poor mother would not have died with the grief of leaving behind a son who was incurably blind. Well, if he was no longer able to console the mother with this hope, couldn't he at least try to convey it to the unhappy survivor, thus affording him a great consolation now that he was so terribly stricken by this new, unexpected misfortune?

And he had proceeded up to the villa.

After a long wait amid the prevailing confusion, he had been greeted by a young woman dressed in black. Blonde, and with a stiff, in fact severe manner, she was the hired companion of the late Marchesa. Dr. Falci had explained to her the reason for his call, which would otherwise have been out of place. At a certain point, with a slight tinge of astonishment that indicated a lack of trust, she had asked him:

"But, in that case, are even young people subject to cataract?"

Falci had looked her in the eye for a moment, then, with an ironic smile more noticeable in his eyes than on his lips, he had replied:

"And why not? Spiritually always, Miss: when they fall in love. But physically also, unfortunately."

She had then cut the conversation short, saying that, under the circumstances in which the Marchese was situated at that moment, it was absolutely impossible to speak to him about anything; but that, when he had calmed down a little, she would tell him about this call and he would surely send for him.

More than three months had gone by: Dr. Giunio Falci had not been sent for.

To tell the truth, on the occasion of his first call the doctor had made a very bad impression on the late Marchesa. Miss Lydia Venturi, who had stayed on as the young Marchese's housekeeper and reader, remembered this clearly. But wouldn't that impression have been different if Falci had right from the start given the Marchesa hopes that her son's recovery was not unlikely? This was a question that Miss Lydia was unwilling to ask herself, and as far as she herself was concerned, she considered the doctor's second call as quackery or worse—coming on the very day the Marchesa had died to declare his dissenting opinion and kindle a hope of that sort.

By this time the young Marchese seemed resigned to his misfortune. His mother having died so suddenly, he had felt another darkness gathering in his soul in addition to that of his blindness: another, much more terrible darkness, in the face of which, it is true, all men are blind. But people with good eyes can at least find distraction from that other darkness by looking at the things around them: he could not. Blind in life, he was now blind in death as well. And into this other darkness, more bare, more cold, more shadowy, his mother had disappeared, silently, leaving him behind alone, in a frightening void.

All at once—he couldn't tell clearly from whom—an infinitely sweet voice had come to him, like a soft, soft light in that double darkness of his. And his entire soul, lost in that frightening void, had seized hold of that voice.

Miss Lydia was no more than a voice to him. Yet it was she who, in the last months, had been closer to his mother than anybody else. And his mother—he recalled this—when speaking to him about her, had expressed great satisfaction with her. Therefore he knew that she was kind, attentive, possessed of perfect good manners, well educated, intelligent; and now, from the attentions she paid him, from the consolations she gave him, he found that she really had all those merits.

From the first day of her employment, Lydia had suspected that the Marchesa Borghi, when hiring her, would not have objected, in her maternal egotism, if her unhappy son had in some way consoled himself in her company: Lydia had been seriously insulted and had forced her natural pride to stiffen into a deportment that was positively severe. But after the misfortune, when, amid his desperate weeping, he had taken hold of her hand, and had leaned his handsome, pale face on it, moaning, "Don't leave me! . . . don't leave me!," she had felt herself overcome by compassion, by tenderness, and had devoted herself to him entirely.

Soon, with the timid but obstinate and heartbreaking curiosity
of the blind, he had begun to torture her. He wanted to "see" her
in his darkness; he wanted her voice to become an image within
him.

At first he posed vague, brief questions. He wanted to tell her
how he pictured her when hearing her read and speak.

"You're blonde, aren't you?"

"Yes . . . "

She *was* blonde; but her hair was somewhat coarse and thin, and
it contrasted strangely with the slightly lusterless color of her skin.
How could she tell him that? And why should she?

"And your eyes, blue?"

"Yes . . . "

Blue they were; but melancholy, sorrowful, too deeply recessed
beneath her serious, sad, prominent brow. How could she tell him
that? And why should she?

Her face was not beautiful, but her body was extremely elegant,
svelte and shapely at the same time. Her hands and her voice were
beautiful, truly beautiful.

Her voice, especially. Of an unutterable sweetness, in contrast to
the melancholy, haughty and sorrowful expression of her face.

She knew how he saw her from the charm of that voice and from
the timid replies she received to his insistent, relentless questions;
and in front of her mirror she made every effort to resemble that
fictitious image he had of her, every effort to see herself the way
he saw her in his darkness. And by this time, even for her, her voice
no longer issued from her own lips, but from those he imagined she
had; and if she laughed, she suddenly had the impression of not
having laughed herself, but rather of having imitated a smile that
was not hers, the smile of that other self who lived within his mind.

All of this caused her a kind of muted torment, it perturbed her:
she felt that she was no longer herself, that she was gradually doing
an injustice to her own self because of the pity the young man
aroused in her. Only pity? No: it was also love now. She was no
longer able to snatch her hand away from his hand, to turn her
face away from his face, if he drew her too closely to him.

"No! like this, no . . . , like this, no . . . "

By this time it was necessary to arrive quickly at a decision which
cost Miss Lydia a long, hard struggle with herself. The young Marchese had no relatives, close or distant, he was his own master and
thus able to do anything he wished or chose. But wouldn't people

say that she was taking advantage of his misfortune in order to get married, to become a Marchesa and rich? Oh, yes, they would surely say that and much more. But, all the same, how could she stay on in that house except on those terms? And wouldn't it be an act of cruelty to abandon that blind man, to deprive him of her loving attentions, through fear of other people's malice? No doubt, it was great good luck for her; but in her conscience she felt that she deserved it because she loved him; in fact, the greatest good luck for her was to be able to love him openly, to be able to say she was his, entirely and eternally his, to be able to devote herself to him exclusively, body and soul. He couldn't see himself: he saw nothing within himself but his own unhappiness; nevertheless, he was handsome—very much so—and as delicate as a little girl; and she, looking at him, delighting in him, without his being aware of it, could think: "There, you're all mine because you don't see yourself and you don't know yourself; because your soul is like a prisoner of your misery and needs me to see, to feel." But wasn't it first necessary, complying with his wishes, to confess to him that she was not like his mental image of her? Wouldn't keeping silent be a deception on her part? Yes, a deception. And yet he was blind, and so he could be satisfied with a heart like hers, devoted and ardent, and with the illusion of beauty. Besides, she was not ugly. And then, a woman who was beautiful, really beautiful, might be able-—who knows?—to deceive him in a much worse way, taking advantage of his misfortune, if he really had need of a loving heart rather than a pretty face, which he could never see.

After several days of anguished uncertainty, the wedding was arranged. It would be celebrated unostentatiously and quickly, just as soon as the sixth month of mourning for his mother had passed.

Therefore she had about a month and a half's time ahead of her to make the necessary preparations as best she could. They were days of tremendous happiness: the hours flew by, divided between her joyful, busy furnishing of their home together and his caresses, from which she would free herself in a mild state of delirium, with gentle force. She wished to preserve that one, most intense, pleasure from the license which their sharing one roof gave to their love, and to save it for their wedding day.

Now there remained little more than a week, when Lydia unexpectedly received the announcement of a visit from Dr. Giunio Falci.

Her first impulse was to answer:

"I'm not home!"

But the blind man, who had heard people talking in low tones, asked:

"Who is it?"

"Dr. Falci," the servant repeated.

"You know," said Lydia, "that doctor your late mother called for a few days before the sad occurrence."

"Oh, yes!" Borghi exclaimed, recalling it to mind. "He gave me a long examination . . . a long one, I remember it clearly, and he said he wanted to come back, in order to . . . "

"Wait," Lydia suddenly interrupted him, in a state of great agitation. "I'll see what he wants."

Dr. Giunio Falci was standing in the center of the reception room, with his large bald head thrown back and his eyes half-closed, and with one hand he was absentmindedly smoothing out the rough little beard on his chin.

"Have a seat, Doctor," said Miss Lydia, who had come in without his noticing.

Falci roused himself, bowed and began saying:

"You will excuse me if . . . "

But she, upset, excited, insisted on saying first:

"You really weren't sent for up to now because . . . "

"My last call was out of place," said Falci, with a light, sarcastic smile on his lips. "But you will forgive me, Miss."

"No . . . Why? Not at all . . . ," said Lydia, blushing.

"You don't know," Falci continued, "how great an interest a poor man concerned with science can take in certain medical cases . . . But I want to tell you the whole truth, Miss: I had forgotten this case of the Marchese Borghi's, even though in my opinion it was very unusual and strange. But yesterday, while chatting about this and that with some friends, I learned about his forthcoming marriage to you, Miss. Is it true?"

Lydia turned pale and nodded affirmatively, in a haughty manner.

"Allow me to congratulate you," Falci added. "But, you see, at that moment, all at once, I remembered. I remembered the diagnosis of glaucoma made by a number of famous colleagues of mine, if I'm not mistaken. A diagnosis that is very easy to explain, in general, I assure you. In fact, I'm certain that if the Marchesa had had those colleagues of mine examine her son at the time I called on him, even they would have said readily that it was no longer proper to speak of a genuine glaucoma. But let that be. I also remembered my second, extremely unfortunate, call, and I thought that you, Miss, at first in the confusion caused by the unexpected death of the Marchesa, and later in the happiness of this new event, had surely forgotten—am I correct?–forgotten . . . "

"No!" said Lydia at that point, contradicting him sharply, in protest against the torture that the doctor's long, poisonous speech was inflicting on her.

"Ah, no?" said Falci.

"No," she repeated, with glowering firmness. "Rather, I remembered how little confidence—actually none at all, forgive me!—the Marchesa had about her son's cure even after your call."

"But I didn't tell the Marchesa," Falci rebutted at once, "that her son's ailment from my point of view . . . "

"It's true, you told that to me," Lydia cut in again. "But I also, like the Marchesa . . . "

"Little confidence—actually none at all, right? It doesn't matter," Falci interrupted in his turn. "But in the meantime you did not inform the Marchese of my coming and the reason for it . . . "

"Not all at once, no."

"And later on?"

"Not then, either. Because . . . "

Dr. Falci raised one hand:

"I understand. After love was born . . . But pardon me, Miss: it's true they say that love is blind; but do you really wish the Marchese's love to be as blind as all that? Blind physically as well?"

Lydia realized that, to combat this man's self-assured, biting coldness, she couldn't make do with the haughty deportment in which she was gradually wrapping herself more and more tightly in order to defend her dignity from an odious suspicion. Nevertheless, she made an effort to contain herself further, and asked with apparent calm:

"You insist on maintaining that the Marchese, with your help, can regain his sight?"

"Don't be hasty, Miss," Falci answered, raising his hand again. "I am not all-powerful. I examined the Marchese's eyes only once, and I thought it proper to rule out glaucoma as a diagnosis absolutely. Now: I think that this conclusion, which may be merely a doubt, or which may be a source of hope, ought to be enough for you if, as I believe, you really have your fiancé's welfare at heart."

"And what if the doubt," Lydia hurriedly replied, in a challenging manner, "could no longer be sustained after your examination, what if the hopes were dashed? Wouldn't you now have uselessly, cruelly perturbed a soul that has already resigned itself to its lot?"

"No, Miss," Falci answered with hard, serious calm. "So little so, that I esteemed it my duty as a physician to come uninvited. Because in this instance, I'd like you to know, I believe I am involved not merely in a medical case but also in a case of conscience."

"You suspect . . . ," Lydia tried to interrupt him, but Falci gave her no time to continue.

"You yourself," he proceeded, "said just now that you failed to inform the Marchese of my call, using an excuse I cannot accept, not because it is insulting to me, but because the confidence or lack of confidence in me ought to come not from you, but from the Marchese, if from anyone. Look, Miss: it may also be obstinacy on my part, I don't deny it; but I tell you that I won't take any payment from the Marchese if he comes to my clinic, where he will have every care and aid that science can offer him, disinterestedly. After this declaration, would it be too much to ask you to announce my call to the Marchese?"

Lydia stood up.

"Wait," Falci then said, getting up also and resuming his customary manner. "I want you to know that I will not say a word to the Marchese about having come that time. In fact, if you like, I'll say that, out of thoughtfulness, you sent for me, before the wedding."

Lydia looked him in the eye undauntedly.

"You shall tell him the truth. No, *I'll* tell him."

"That you didn't believe me."

"Exactly."

Falci shrugged his shoulders, smiled.

"It might do you harm. And I wouldn't want that. But if you wanted to postpone my call until after the wedding—look, I would be equally willing to come back."

"No," said Lydia, speaking more with her gesture than with her voice. Stifled by her agitation, her face flushed with shame caused by that apparent generosity of the doctor, she signaled with her hand for him to come with her.

Silvio Borghi was waiting impatiently in his room.

"Here is Dr. Falci, Silvio," said Lydia, entering, trembling all over. "Downstairs we cleared up a misunderstanding. You remember, don't you, that on his first call the Doctor said he wanted to come back?"

"Yes," answered Borghi. "I remember very well, Doctor."

"What you don't know yet," continued Lydia, "is that he did in fact come back, on the very morning when your mother's sad death occurred. And he spoke with me and told me that he believed your ailment was not really what so many other doctors had declared it to be, and that, in his opinion, therefore, it was not at all unlikely that you could be cured. I told you nothing about it."

"Because, you see, your fiancée," Dr. Falci hastened to add, "seeing that it was a doubt that I expressed in very vague terms at that moment, considered it, more than anything else, as a consolation I wished to offer, and didn't attach much importance to it."

"That is what I said, not what you think," Lydia replied intrepidly. "Dr. Falci, Silvio, suspected what is actually the truth, that I told you nothing about his second call; and he was kind enough to come entirely on his own, before the wedding, to offer you his treatment without any remuneration. Now, Silvio, you are free to think, as he does, that I wanted you to stay blind to get you to marry me."

"What are you saying, Lydia?" the blind man exclaimed with a start.

"Oh, yes," she continued at once, with a strange laugh. "And even that may be true, because, in fact, that's the only way I could become your . . . "

"What are you saying?" Borghi repeated, interrupting her.

"You'll see for yourself, Silvio, if Dr. Falci succeeds in restoring your sight. I'll leave you now."

"Lydia! Lydia!" Borghi called.

But she had already gone out, slamming the door behind her violently. She went and threw herself on her bed, bit the pillow in her rage and at first broke out into uncontrollable sobbing. When the first fury of her tears had abated, she remained dumbfounded and as if horrified in the face of her own conscience. It seemed to her that everything the doctor had said to her, in that cold and biting way of his, she had already said to herself for some time; or, rather, someone inside her had said it; and she had pretended not to hear. Yes, all along, all along she had remembered Dr. Falci, and every time his image had surfaced in her mind, like the ghost of a remorse, she had suppressed it with an insult: "Charlatan!" Because—how could she go on denying it now?—she wished, truly wished her Silvio to remain blind. His blindness was the indispensable condition for his love. For, if he should regain his sight tomorrow, handsome as he was, young, rich, a nobleman, why would he marry her? Out of gratitude? Out of pity? Ah, for no other reason! And, in that case, no, no! And even if *he* were willing, *she* wouldn't be; how could she accept that?—she who loved him and wanted him for no other reason; she who saw in his misfortune the reason for her love and almost the excuse for it in the face of other people's malice. Can one, then, make compromises with one's own conscience that way, without realizing it, to the point of committing a crime, to the point of founding one's own happiness on someone else's suffering? To be perfectly honest, at that time she had not believed that he, her enemy, could perform the miracle of restoring her Silvio's sight; she didn't believe it even now; but why had she remained silent? Was it really because she had not thought it proper to lend credence to that doctor, or wasn't it rather because the doubt the doctor had expressed, which would have been like a ray of hope for Silvio, would have meant death instead for her, the death of her love, if it later proved to be true? Even now she could believe that her love would have been sufficient to compensate that blind man for the loss of his sight; she could believe that, even if by some miracle he now regained his sight, neither that supreme blessing, nor all the pleasures he could buy himself with his wealth, nor the love of some other woman, could compensate him for the loss of *her* love. But these were reasons for herself, not for him. If she had gone to him and said, "Silvio, you have to choose between the joy of seeing and my love," he surely would have replied, "And why do you want to leave me blind?" Because only this way, that is, on the condition of his misfortune, was her happiness possible.

All at once she stood up, as if in answer to a sudden call. Was the examination still going on in that other room? What was the doctor saying? What was *he* thinking? She was tempted to tiptoe over and eavesdrop behind that door she herself had closed; but she restrained herself. There you had it: she was left behind the door; she herself, with her own hands, had closed it on herself, forever. But could she really accept that man's poisonous offers? He had gone so far as to propose postponing his call until after the wedding.—If she had accepted . . . No! No! She felt herself tighten up with disgust, with nausea. What a hateful deal that would have been! The most loathsome of deceptions! And later on? Contempt in place of love . . .

She heard the door open; she shuddered; instinctively she ran to the corridor through which Falci had to pass.

"I made up for your excessive frankness, Miss," he said coldly. "I have confirmed my diagnosis. The Marchese will come to my clinic tomorrow morning. Meanwhile, go to him, go, he's waiting for you. Goodbye."

She stood there annihilated, drained; she watched him go all the way to the door at the far end of the corridor; then she heard Silvio's voice calling her from his room. She felt all confused, dizzy; she was on the point of falling; she put her hands to her face to hold back her tears; she hastened toward him.

He was sitting and awaiting her with open arms; he hugged her to himself with tremendous strength, shouting his happiness in short, choppy phrases, saying that it was for her alone that he wanted to regain his sight, to see her face, to see his beautiful, sweet bride; for her!

"You're crying? Why? But I'm crying, too, see? Oh, what joy! I'll see you . . . I'll see! I'll see!"

Every word was death to her; so much so that, happy as he was, he realized that her tears were not the same as his, and he then started to tell her that surely—oh, but surely—not even he, on a day like that one, would have believed what the doctor said, and so, forget it, enough now! What was she still thinking about? Today was a holiday! Away with all sorrows! Away with all thoughts, except one: that his happiness would now be complete because he would see his bride. Now she would have more leisure, more time to furnish their home together; and it had to be beautiful as a dream, that home, which would be the first thing he saw. Yes, he promised that he would leave the clinic with his eyes bandaged, and that he would open them there, for the first time, in his home.

"Speak to me! Speak to me! Don't let me go on speaking alone!"

"Are you getting tired?"

"No . . . Ask me again, 'Are you getting tired?' with that voice of yours. Let me kiss it, here, on your lips, that voice of yours . . . "

"Yes . . . "

"And speak, now; tell me how you'll furnish it for me, our home."

"How?"

"Yes, I haven't asked you anything yet up to now. But no, I don't want to know anything, not even now. You will take care of it. For me it will be a marvel, an enchantment . . . But I will see nothing at first: only you! only you!"

She resolutely stifled her anguished weeping, made her face completely cheerful, and there kneeling in front of him, with him bending over her, in her embrace, she began speaking to him of her love, practically in his ear, with that voice of hers, sweeter and more bewitching than ever. But when he, in rapture, held her tight and threatened never to let her go again, at that moment she freed herself and stood straight up, as if proud of a victory over herself. There! Even now, she would have been able to tie him to her indissolubly. But no! Because she loved him.

All that day, till late at night, she intoxicated him with that voice of hers, self-assured because he was still there, in his darkness; in the darkness in which hope was already flaring up, as beautiful as the image he had formed of her.

The next morning she insisted on accompanying him in the carriage up to the clinic and, as she left him there, she told him she would get right to work, right away, like an industrious swallow building her nest.

"You'll see!"

For two days, in terrible anxiety, she awaited the result of the operation. When she heard it was successful, she waited a little longer, in the empty house; she furnished it for him lovingly. In his exultation he wanted to see her, if only for a moment, but she sent a message asking him to be patient for a few more days; if she wasn't hurrying over, it was to avoid exciting him; it was against the doctor's orders . . .

"Really? Well, in that case she would have come . . . "

She gathered up her possessions, and the day before he left the clinic, she departed without anyone knowing, in order to remain, at least in his memory, a voice, which perhaps, now that he had emerged from his darkness, he would seek on many lips, in vain.

THE FLY

Out of breath, panting—when they were below the village, which sits with its densely packed chalky little houses on the blue-clay plateau—to save time they climbed up the slippery slope, making use of their hands, because their large, coarse hobnailed shoes were sliding, damn it!

The women, closely gathered and talking loudly in front of the little fountain, with their terra-cotta pitchers under their arms, turned around and fell silent in alarm when they saw those two men coming, overheated, purple in the face, drenched with sweat, worn out. Say, weren't those two the Tortorici brothers? Yes, Neli and Saro Tortorici. Poor things! Poor things! They were unrecognizable in that state. What had happened to them? Why that desperate haste?

Neli, the younger of the brothers, totally exhausted, had stopped to catch his breath and answer the women's questions; but Saro dragged him away with him by one arm.

"Giurlannu Zarù, our cousin!" Neli then said, turning around, and raised one hand in a gesture of benediction.

The women broke out into exclamations of sympathy and horror, and one loudly asked:

"Who did it?"

"Nobody, God!" Neli shouted from the distance.

They turned a corner and ran to the little village square, where the house of the municipal doctor stood.

The physician in question, Sidoro Lopiccolo, in his shirt sleeves, with his chest exposed, with a rough beard of at least ten days' growth on his flabby cheeks, unkempt, with swollen, watery, sunken eyes, was moving about through the rooms, dragging his slippers, and carrying in his arms a poor little sick girl—nothing but skin and bones, with a sallow complexion—about nine years old. His wife, bedridden for eleven months, unable to help; six little children in the house—besides the one he was holding in his arms, who was the eldest—all in tatters, dirty, running wild; the whole house upside down, a ruin; broken dishes, rinds, the garbage piled on the floor; broken chairs, bottomless armchairs, beds that hadn't been made for who knows how long, with the blankets in shreds, because the boys enjoyed playing war on the beds with the pillows as weapons, the little dears! The only thing still intact, in a room that had once been the little parlor, was an enlarged photographic portrait hung on the wall: the portrait of him, Dr. Sidoro Lopiccolo, when he was a young man, recently graduated: handsome, well dressed, fresh-looking and smiling.

To this portrait he now made his way, with flopping slippers; he bared his yellow teeth at it, in a frightening leer; he shook his head; he showed it his sick daughter:

"Sisinello, Sisinè!"

Sisinello, that's what his mother used to call him as a pet name back then; his mother, who expected great things of him, the favorite son, the golden pillar, the banner of the household.

"Sisinello, Sisinè!"

He greeted the two farmhands like a rabid mastiff:

"What do you want?"

It was Saro Tortorici who spoke, short of breath, with his cap in his hand:

"Doctor, there's a poor man, our cousin, who's dying . . . "

"Good for him! Ring the church bells to celebrate!" the doctor shouted.

"No, sir . . . He's dying just like that, nobody knows what from," the other man continued. "On the Montelusa property, in a stable."

The doctor took a step backward and exploded in fury:

"At Montelusa?"

From the village it was a good seven miles along the road. And what a road!

"Yes, sir, hurry, hurry, for mercy's sake!" Tortorici begged. "He's black, like a liver! So swollen up, it's frightening. Please!"

"But how, on foot?" the doctor howled. "Ten miles on foot? You're crazy! A mule! I want a mule. Did you bring one?"

"I'll run right over and get one," Tortorici hastened to reply. "I'll borrow one."

"In that case," said Neli, the younger brother, "I'll dash over in the meantime and get a shave."

The doctor turned around and looked at him as if he wanted to eat him up alive.

"It's Sunday, sir," Neli apologized, smiling in confusion. "I'm engaged."

"Ah, you're engaged?" the doctor then sneered, beside himself. "If that's the case, take this one!"

So saying, he dumped his sick daughter into his arms; then, one by one, he took the other little ones who had crowded around him and furiously shoved them between his knees:

"And this one! And this one! And this one! And this one! Fool! Fool! Fool!"

He turned his back on him, started to leave, but came back again, took back the sick girl and shouted at the two:

"Go away! Get the mule! I'll be right with you."

Neli Tortorici resumed smiling as he went down the stairs behind his brother. He was twenty; his fiancée, Luzza, sixteen: a rose. Seven children? That's not many! He wanted twelve. And to support them he would rely on nothing but that pair of arms, good ones, that God had given him. Cheerfully, as always. Working and singing, all in a professional way: his mattock and his song. It wasn't for nothing they called him Liolà, the poet. He smiled even at the air he breathed, because he felt loved by everyone, because of his helpfulness and good nature, because of his unfailing good humor, because of his youthful good looks. The sun had not yet managed to tan his skin, to wither the beautiful golden blonde of his curly hair, which plenty of women would have envied him, all those women who blushed in their agitation if he looked at them in a certain way with those extremely vivid blue eyes.

That day, he was fundamentally less afflicted by the case of his cousin Zarù than by the sulky treatment he would receive from his Luzza, who for six days had been yearning for that Sunday to spend a little time with him. But could he in all conscience shirk that duty of Christian charity? Poor Giurlannu! He was engaged, too! What a disaster, all of a sudden like that! He was knocking down the almonds out there, on the Lopes farm at Montelusa. The morning before, Saturday, the weather had begun to threaten rain; but there seemed to be no imminent danger of its falling. Toward noon, however, Lopes said: "Things happen fast; I wouldn't want my almonds to lie on the ground, exposed to the rain." And he had ordered the women who were gathering them to go up to the storehouse and shell them. "You," he said, addressing the men who were knocking down the nuts, among them Neli and Saro Tortorici, "you, if you want, go up, too, with the women to shell them." Giurlannu Zarù said: "Fine, but will I still get my full day's wages, twenty-

five *soldi*?" "No, half-pay," said Lopes; "I'll count it in when I pay
you; for the rest of the day, the rate is half a *lira*, like the women."
What an outrage! Why? Maybe there wasn't enough work for the
men to do and earn a full day's pay? It wasn't raining; in fact, it
didn't rain all that day, or that night. "Half a *lira*, like the women?
said Giurlannu Zarù. "I wear pants. Pay me for the half day at the
rate of twenty-five *soldi*, and I'll leave."

He didn't leave; he stayed there waiting until evening for his
cousins, who consented to shell almonds, at the rate of half a *lira*,
along with the women. At a certain point, however, tired of standing
around idle and looking on, he had gone into a nearby stable to
catch a nap, asking the work crew to wake him up when it was time
to go.

They had been knocking down almonds for a day and a half,
but not many had been gathered. The women suggested shelling
all of them that very evening, working late and staying there to
sleep for the rest of the night, then making their way back up to
the village the next morning, getting up while it was still dark. And
that's what they did. Lopes brought them boiled beans and two
bottles of wine. At midnight, when the shelling was over, all of
them, men and women, went out to sleep in the open air on the
threshing floor, where the straw that had been left there was wet
with dew, as if it really had rained.

"Liolà, sing!"

And he, Neli, had begun singing, all at once. The moon passed
in and out of a dense tangle of little white and black clouds; and
the moon was Luzza's face, smiling and darkening in accordance
with the vicissitudes—now sad, now happy—of love.

Giurlannu Zarù had remained in the stable. Before dawn, Saro
had gone to awaken him and had found him there, swollen and
black, with a raging fever.

That is the story Neli Tortorici told there, at the barber's; at a
certain point the barber, his attention wandering, nicked him with
the razor. A tiny cut, near his chin, that wasn't even visible—forget
it! Neli didn't even have time to feel it, because Luzza had appeared
at the barber's door with her mother and Mita Lumìa, Giurlannu
Zarù's poor fiancée, who was yelling and weeping in despair.

It took a lot of talking to make the poor girl understand that she
couldn't go all the way to Montelusa to see her fiancé: she would
see him before evening, as soon as they brought him up as best

they could. They were joined by Saro, shouting loudly that the doctor was already mounted and didn't want to wait any longer. Neli drew Luzza aside and begged her to be patient: he would return before evening and would "tell her all sorts of nice things."

In fact, even sad things like this are nice, for an engaged couple who say them to each other while holding hands and looking into each other's eyes.

What a godforsaken road! There were some cliffs that made Dr. Lopiccolo see death before his eyes, even though Saro on one side and Neli on the other were leading the mule by the halter.

From the heights one could make out the entire vast countryside, all plains and dales; planted with grain, olive groves and almond groves; already yellow with fields of stubble and flecked with black here and there by land-clearing fires; in the background one could make out the sea, of a harsh blue. The mulberry, carob, cypress and olive trees still retained their various shades of perennial green; the tops of the almond trees had already thinned out. All around, in the extensive circle of the horizon, there was a sort of veil of wind. But the heat was overpowering; the sun split the stones. From time to time, from beyond the dusty hedges of prickly pear, there was heard the call of a lark or the chatter of a magpie, making the doctor's mule prick up its ears.

"Bad mule! Bad mule!" he would then lament.

In order to keep his gaze fixed on those ears, he didn't even pay attention to the sunshine striking him from the front, and he left his wretched open parasol leaning on his shoulder.

"Don't be afraid, sir, *we're* here," the Tortorici brothers encouraged him.

To tell the truth, the doctor ought not to have been afraid. But he said that he feared for his children. Didn't he have to save his skin for the sake of those seven unfortunates?

To distract him, the Tortoricis started telling him about the bad crops: not much wheat, not much barley, not many beans. As for the almond trees, it's well known—they don't always form good nuts: one year they're chock-full, the next year not. They wouldn't even mention the olives: the fog had destroyed them as they were developing. Nor could the farmers make up their losses with the grape harvest, because all the vineyards in the region were stricken by blight.

"Fine way to cheer me up!" the doctor would say every once in a while, shaking his head.

After two hours on the road, all topics of conversation were exhausted. Each man was shut up within himself. The road was flat for a long stretch and there, on the deep layer of whitish dust, the conversation was now carried on between the four hooves of the mule and the big hobnailed shoes of the two farmhands. Liolà, at a certain point, began to sing listlessly in low tones; he soon stopped. Not a living soul was to be found on the road, because all the countryfolk were in the village on Sundays, some in church, some shopping, some for amusement. Perhaps out there, at Montelusa, nobody had remained beside Giurlannu Zarù, who was dying all alone; that is, if he was still alive, poor guy.

In fact, they did find him alone, in the little musty stable, stretched out on a low wall: livid, swollen up, unrecognizable, but still alive!

He was breathing stertorously.

Through the barred window, near the manger, the sun came in and struck his face, which no longer seemed human: his nose had been swallowed up in the swelling; his lips were horribly puffed up. And from those lips issued the heavy breathing, intensified, like a snarl. In his thick, curly hair, dark as a Moor's, a wisp of straw glistened in the sunlight.

The three men stopped for a while to stare at him, frightened and seemingly immobilized by the horror of that sight. The mule, sputtering, pawed the cobbled floor of the stable. Then Saro Tortorici went over to the dying man and called to him affectionately:

"Giurlà, Giurlà, the doctor is here."

Neli went to tie the mule to the manger, near which, on the wall, was the seeming shadow of another animal, the trace of the donkey that resided in that stable and had impressed his outline on it by dint of rubbing up against it.

Giurlannu Zarù, on being called again, stopped his heavy breathing; he tried to open his eyes, which were bloodshot, circled with black and full of fear; he opened his horrendous mouth and groaned, as if burning inside.

"I'm dying!"

"No, no," Saro quickly said to him in anguish. "The doctor is here. We brought him. See him?"

"Take me to the village!" Zarù begged. "Oh, Mother!"

"Yes, look, we've got the mule here!" Saro at once replied.

"But I'll even carry you there in my arms, Giurlà," said Neli, running up and bending over him. "Don't lose courage!"

Giurlannu Zarù turned toward Neli's voice, looked at him for a while with those fear-provoking eyes, then moved one arm and took hold of his belt.

"You, Handsome? You?"

"Yes, me; be brave! You're crying? Don't cry, Giurlà, don't cry . . . It's nothing!"

And he placed a hand on his chest, which was shaken by the sobs that were stuck in his throat. Choking, Zarù shook his head furiously, then raised one hand, took Neli by the nape of his neck and drew him toward himself:

"We were supposed to get married at the same time . . . "

"And we *will* get married at the same time, have no doubts!" said Neli, removing his hand, which had clasped his neck tightly.

Meanwhile the doctor was observing the dying man. It was clear: a case of anthrax.

"Tell me, do you recall being bitten by any insect?"

"No," Zarù indicated by shaking his head.

"Insect?" asked Saro.

The doctor explained the disease to those two uneducated men as best he could. Some animal must have died of anthrax in that vicinity. Insects—who knows how many?—had lighted on the carcass, which had been thrown away into some ravine; one of them could have transmitted the disease to Zarù.

While the doctor was speaking, Zarù had turned his face to the wall. No one knew it, but all the same death was still there; so small that it could hardly have been descried if anyone had intentionally looked for it. It was a fly, there on the wall, seemingly immobile; but, if you looked closely, now it was projecting its little mouth-tube and pumping, now it was rapidly cleaning its two thin front feet, rubbing them together, as if in contentment. Zarù caught sight of it and stared at it.

A fly . . .

It might have been that one or another one . . . Who knows? Because now, hearing the doctor talk, he thought he remembered. Yes, the day before, when he had lain down there to sleep, waiting for his cousins to finish shelling Lopes' almonds, a fly had bothered him terribly . . . Could it be this one? He saw it take flight and followed its movements with his eyes. There! it had landed on Neli's cheek. From his cheek, softly, softly, it was now moving, in a broken line, to his chin, right up to the razor scratch, and there it dug in, voraciously.

Giurlannu Zarù kept looking at it for a while intently, with concentration. Then, through his catarrhal panting, he asked in a cavernous voice:

"Could it be a fly?"

"A fly? Why not?" the doctor replied.

Giurlannu Zarù said nothing more: he resumed staring at that fly, which Neli, as if dazed by the doctor's words, failed to shoo away. He, Zarù, was paying no attention to the doctor's speech, but was pleased that, with his talking, he was engrossing his cousin's attention to such an extent that Neli remained as motionless as a statue and paid no heed to the annoyance that fly was causing him. Oh, if it were only the same one! Yes, then they really would get married at the same time! He had been seized by a sullen envy, an unspoken ferocious jealousy of that young cousin, so strong and healthy, for whom life remained full of promise—life, which suddenly was running out for *him* . . .

All at once Neli, as if he had felt himself bitten, raised one hand, drove away the fly and with his fingers began to pinch his chin, where the little cut was, turning toward Zarù, who was looking at him and had opened his horrendous lips, as if in a monstrous smile. They looked at each other in that way for a while. Then Zarù said, as if not meaning to:

"The fly . . . "

Neli didn't understand and bent down his head to listen.

"What are you saying?"

"The fly . . . ," he repeated.

"Which one? Where?" asked Neli, in alarm, looking at the doctor.

"There, where you're scratching. I'm sure of it!" said Zarù.

Neli showed the doctor the tiny wound in his chin.

"What's wrong with me? It itches . . . "

The doctor looked at him, frowning; then, as if he wanted to examine him more closely, he led him out of the stables. Saro followed them.

What happened next? Giurlannu Zarù waited, waited a long time, with an anxiety that irritated all his insides. He heard a confused sound of talking outside. All of a sudden, Saro came back into the stable furiously, took the mule and, without even turning around to look at him, went out, moaning:

"Ah, my Neluccio! Ah, my Neluccio!"

Was it true, then? And look, were they abandoning him there, like a dog? . . . He tried to raise himself on one elbow and called out twice:

"Saro . . . Saro . . . "

Silence. Nobody. He couldn't support himself any longer on his elbow, he fell back into a recumbent position and for a while he seemed to be rooting and grubbing around, in order not to hear the silence of the countryside, which terrified him. Suddenly he began to wonder whether he had dreamed the whole thing, whether he had had that bad dream in his feverish state; but, when he turned to the wall, he saw the fly there again. Now it was projecting its little mouth-tube and pumping, now it was rapidly cleaning its two thin front feet, rubbing them together, as if in contentment.

THE OIL JAR

A bumper crop of olives, too, that year. Productive trees, laden down the year before, had all borne firm fruit, in spite of the fog that had stifled them when in blossom.

Zirafa, who had a fair number of them on his farm Le Quote at Primosole, foreseeing that the five old glazed ceramic oil jars he had in his cellar wouldn't be enough to hold all the oil from the new harvest, had ordered a sixth, larger one in advance from Santo Stefano di Camastra, where they were made: as tall as a man's chest, beautiful, big-bellied and majestic, it would be the "abbess" of the five others.

Needless to say, he had litigated even with the kiln operator there over this jar. And with whom did Don[1] Lollò Zirafa fail to litigate? Over any trifle, even over a crumb of stone that had fallen from the perimeter wall, even over a wisp of straw, he would go to court. And by dint of all those legal documents and lawyers' fees, summonsing this man and that and always paying the costs for everyone, he had half ruined himself.

They said that his legal adviser, tired of seeing him showing up on his mule two or three times a week, in order to get rid of him had made him a present of a tiny, tiny little gem of a book, like a missal—the law code—so that he could rack his brains searching out for himself the legal basis for the lawsuits he wished to institute.

Before that, all those he had quarrels with, to make fun of him, used to shout at him: "Saddle the mule!" Now, instead, they said to him: "Consult the handbook!"

And Don Lollò would answer:

"I sure will, and I'll annihilate you, sons of bitches!"

That new jar—for which he had paid four good *onze*[2] in hard cash—while awaiting the right spot to be found for it in the cellar, was temporarily stored in the grape-pressing shed. A jar like that had never been seen: it could hold at least two hundred liters.

---

[1] A term of respect for a landowner, nobleman or other prominent member of society in Sicily.

[2] *Onza*, or *oncia*, an old Sicilian monetary unit.

46

Stored in that dark cave, reeking of must and that acrid, raw smell that lurks in places without air or light, it was pitiful to behold. Some serious misfortune had to be suffered on its account, everyone told him. But Don Lollò, at that warning, would shrug his shoulders.

Two days earlier they had begun to knock down the olives, and he was in a vile temper, because he didn't know where to turn first, since the people with the fertilizer to be deposited in heaps here and there for the new season's bean crop had also arrived with their laden mules. On the one hand, he would have liked to be present while that steady parade of animals was being unloaded; on the other hand, he didn't want to leave the men who were knocking down the olives; and he went around cursing like a Turk and threatening to annihilate this man and that, if a single well-grown olive should be missing, just as if he had already counted them all, one by one, on the trees; or if each pile of manure wasn't as high as all the rest. With his homely white hat, in his shirt sleeves, his chest bare, his face all red, dripping all over with sweat, he kept running back and forth, rolling his wolflike eyes and furiously rubbing his shaven cheeks, on which the heavy beard grew back again almost at the very moment it was shaved off.

Now, at the end of the third day, three of the farmhands who had been knocking down the olives, coming into the wine-press shed to put away the ladders and the poles, stood stock still at the sight of the beautiful new jar, split almost in two. A large strip in front had been detached, all in one piece, as if someone —"whack!"—had cut it clean through with his hatchet, across the widest part of its belly, all the way down.

"I'm dying! I'm dying! I'm dying!" exclaimed one of the three, almost tonelessly, beating his chest with one hand.

"Who did it?" asked the second.

And the third:

"Oh, mother! Who is going to face Don Lollò now? Who's going to tell him? Honestly, the new jar! Oh, what a shame!"

The first man, the most frightened of them all, suggested that they immediately close the shutters of the door again and go away as quietly as possible, leaving the ladders and poles outside leaning up against the wall. But the second man vigorously objected:

"Are you crazy? With Don Lollò? He's liable to believe that *we* broke it. We stay right here!"

He went out in front of the shed and, using his hands to amplify his voice, called:

"Don Lollò! Oh, Don Lollòoo!"

The Don was down the hillside over there with the men who were unloading the fertilizer, and was gesticulating furiously in his accustomed manner, from time to time pulling his ugly white hat down over his eyes with both hands. Every once in a while, he pulled it down so hard that he could no longer wrench it off his neck and forehead. In the sky the last flames of the sunset were already going out, and amid the peace that descended onto the countryside with the shades of evening and the pleasant coolness, the gestures of that permanently enraged man stood out conspicuously.

"Don Lollò! Oh, Don Lollòoo!"

When he arrived and saw the havoc, it seemed he would go mad; first he hurled himself at those three men: he seized one of them by the throat and pinned him to the wall, shouting:

"Blood of the Madonna, you'll pay for this!"

Seized in his turn by the other two, their earth-colored, parched, brutish faces distorted by excitement, he turned his violent rage against himself, flung his ugly hat to the ground, and beat his head and cheeks for a long time, stamping his feet and bawling in the fashion of people mourning a dead relative:

"The new jar! Four *onze's* worth of jar! Not even used once!"

He wanted to know who had broken it! Did it break by itself? Someone must have broken it, out of meanness or out of envy! But when? How? There were no visible signs of violence! Could it have arrived broken from the potter's shop? No! It rang like a bell!

As soon as the farmhands saw that his first fury had abated, they started urging him to calm down. The jar could be repaired. You see, it wasn't damaged badly. Just a single piece was broken. A competent tinker could fix it, make it as good as new. And Uncle Dima Licasi was the very man; he had discovered a miraculous resin cement, the secret formula for which he guarded jealously: a cement that couldn't even be broken by a hammer, once it had taken hold. There. If Don Lollò was willing, tomorrow, at the crack of dawn, Uncle Dima Licasi would come and, before you knew it, the jar would be better than before.

Don Lollò said no to those exhortations: it was all useless; there was no longer any way to put things right; but finally he allowed himself to be persuaded, and the next day, at dawn, punctually, Uncle Dima Licasi showed up at Primosole with his tool chest on his back.

He was a crooked old man, with knotty arthritic joints, like an old stump of Saracen[3] olive tree. To wrench a word out of his mouth you needed a hook. It was haughtiness, that taciturnity, it was sadness rooted in that misshapen body of his; it was also a lack of belief that others could understand and rightly appreciate his deserts as an inventor who had not yet received any patent. He wanted the facts to speak for themselves, did Uncle Dima Licasi. And thus he had to be constantly on his guard so that his secret formula for making that miraculous cement wasn't stolen.

"Show it to me," Don Lollò said to him, first off, after looking him up and down for some time in distrust.

Uncle Dima shook his head in refusal, full of dignity.

"You'll see when it's done."

"But will it work?"

Uncle Dima put his tool chest on the ground and took out of it a tattered and faded cotton handkerchief, all rolled up; he unfolded it; he religiously drew out of it a pair of eyeglasses with the bridge and side pieces broken and tied with string; he put them on and began to examine attentively the jar, which had been brought out into the open air, on the threshing floor. He said:

"It will work."

"But with the cement alone," Zirafa laid down as a condition, "I wouldn't feel safe. I want rivets as well."

"In that case I'm leaving," Uncle Dima replied tersely, putting his tool chest behind his back again.

Don Lollò caught him by one arm.

"Where are you off to? Sir Pig, is that how you deal with people? Look, he puts on airs as if he were Charlemagne! A down-and-out, miserable, ugly tinker, that's what you are, you donkey, and you ought to follow orders! I've got to put oil in there, and oil oozes out, you dumb animal! A crack a mile long, with nothing but cement? I want rivets. Cement and rivets. I'm the one giving the orders."

Uncle Dima shut his eyes, pressed his lips together and shook his head. They were all the same! He was denied the pleasure of doing a clean job, in a conscientious, artisanlike manner, and thus furnishing a proof of the powers of his cement.

"If the jar," he said, "doesn't ring again like a bell . . . "

"No, no!" Don Lollò interrupted him. "Rivets! I'm paying for cement and rivets. How much are you asking?"

---

[3] That is, planted by the former Arab occupants of Sicily.

"If it's with the cement only . . . "

"Damn it, what a thick head!" exclaimed Zirafa. "What have I been saying? I told you I want rivets in it. We'll settle up when the job is done: I have no time to waste with you."

And he went off to keep an eye on his men.

Uncle Dima started working, swollen with anger and vexation. And his anger and vexation grew with every drill hole he made in the jar and in the detached piece for the iron wire of the riveting to pass through. He accompanied the whirring of the bit with grunts that became gradually more frequent and louder; and his face became greener with bile and his eyes more and more sharp and inflamed with rage. When that first operation was over, he furiously hurled the drill into the tool chest; he fitted the detached piece to the jar to make sure that the holes were equidistant and matching, then with his pincers he snipped the iron wire into as many small lengths as there were rivets to insert, and he called as an assistant one of the farmhands who were knocking down olives.

"Cheer up, Uncle Dima," that man said to him, seeing his face all upset.

Uncle Dima raised one hand in a furious gesture. He opened the tin box that contained the cement, and raised it to the sky, shaking it, as if to offer it to God, inasmuch as mankind refused to acknowledge its efficacy: then with a finger he began to spread it all around the edges of the detached piece and along the crack; he took the pincers and the previously prepared small lengths of iron wire, and thrust himself into the open belly of the jar.

"From inside?" asked the farmhand, to whom he had given the detached piece to support.

He didn't reply. With a gesture he ordered him to fit that piece to the jar, as he himself had done shortly before, and stayed inside. Before beginning to insert the rivets:

"Pull!" he said to the farmhand from inside the jar, in a tearful voice. "Pull with all your might! See if it comes off again! The devil take anyone who doesn't believe it! And bang on it, bang on it! Hear how it sounds, even with me inside here? Go and tell that to your fine master."

"The man on top gives the orders, Uncle Dima," the farmhand sighed, "and the man on the bottom is damned! Put in the rivets, put in the rivets."

And Uncle Dima began passing every piece of iron wire through the two adjacent holes, one on either side of the mend; and with

the pincers he twisted the two ends. It took about an hour to pass
them all through. He sweated rivers inside the jar. As he worked,
he quietly lamented his evil fortune. And the farmhand, outside,
kept consoling him.

"Now help me get out," Uncle Dima finally said.

But as wide as it was around the belly, that's how narrow that jar
was at the neck. That farmhand had had a true premonition! Uncle
Dima, in his rage, had paid no attention. Now, try and try again as
he would, he found no way of getting back out. And the farmhand,
instead of helping him—there he was, doubled up with laughter.
Imprisoned, imprisoned there, in the jar he himself had repaired,
and which now—there was no other way—to let him out, would
have to be broken again and for good.

The laughter and shouting brought Don Lollò onto the scene.
Uncle Dima, inside the jar, was like a maddened cat.

"Get me out!" he was howling. "For God's sake, I want to get
out! Right away! Help me out!"

At first Don Lollò just stood there stunned. He couldn't believe
it.

"But how? Inside? He riveted himself up inside?"

He went over to the jar and shouted to the old man:

"Help? And what help can I give you? Stupid old man, how could
you? Shouldn't you have taken the measurements first? Come on,
try, stick out an arm, like that! And your head, come on . . . no,
easy does it! What? What have you done? And the jar, now? Keep
calm! Keep calm! Keep calm!" he started to advise everyone around
him, as if it were the others who were losing their composure and
not he. "My head is on fire! Keep calm! This is a new case . . . The
mule!"

He tapped on the jar with his knuckles. It really did ring like a
bell.

"Beautiful! As good as new . . . Wait!" he said to the prisoner.
"Go saddle my mule!" he ordered the farmhand; and, scratching
his forehead with his fingers, he continued saying to himself: "But
just look at what happens to me! This isn't a jar. It's a contrivance
of the devil! Easy! Easy there!"

And he ran over to steady the jar, in which Uncle Dima was
violently writhing like a trapped animal.

"A new case, my good man, which my lawyer needs to settle! I
don't trust myself. I'll be back in a flash, be patient! It's in your
own interests . . . Meanwhile, be still! Keep calm! I look after my

people. And before all else, in order to have a just claim, I do my duty. Here: I'm paying you for the job, I'm paying you for the day's work. Three *lire*. Is that enough?"

"I don't want a thing!" shouted Uncle Dima. "I want to get out!"

"You *will* get out. But in the meantime I'm paying you. Here, three *lire*."

He took them out of his vest pocket and threw them into the jar. Then he asked, solicitously:

"Have you had lunch? A lunch over here, right away! You don't want any? Throw it to the dogs! It's enough for me that I gave it to you."

He ordered them to give the tinker lunch; he climbed into the saddle, and trotted off to town. Everyone who saw him thought he was going to commit himself to the insane asylum, from the extent and strangeness of his gesticulations, while talking to himself.

Luckily he didn't have to sit and wait at the lawyer's office; but he did have to wait a good while for the lawyer to stop laughing, once he had explained the case. He was annoyed at the laughter.

"But, tell me, what is there to laugh about? It doesn't affect *you!* The jar is mine!"

But the lawyer kept on laughing and wanted him to tell the whole story over again, just as it happened, so he could have another laugh. Inside, huh? He riveted himself up inside? And *he*, Don Lollò, what did he want to do? Kee. . . to kee. . . to keep him in there . . . ha, ha, ha . . . to keep him in there so as not to lose the jar?

"Do I have to lose it?" asked Zirafa with clenched fists. "The loss and the shame?"

"But do you know what this is called?" the lawyer said. "It's called 'illegal confinement.'"

"Confinement? And who confined him?" exclaimed Zirafa. "He confined himself! How am I to blame?"

The lawyer then explained to him that there were two cases. On the one hand, he, Don Lollò, was obliged to release the prisoner at once so as not to be liable to the charge of "illegal confinement"; on the other hand, the tinker was answerable for the damage he was causing through his lack of professionalism and his carelessness.

"Ah!" said Zirafa, with a sigh of relief. "By paying me for the jar!"

"Not so fast!" the lawyer remarked. "It's not as if it were new, keep that in mind!"

"And why not?"

"Why, because it was broken!"

"No, sir!" Zirafa rebutted. "Now it's whole. Better than whole, he says so himself! And if I now break it again, I won't be able to have it mended again. It's a lost jar, counselor!"

The lawyer assured him that this would be taken into account, by demanding a payment equal to the jar's value in its present condition.

"In fact," he advised him, "have it appraised in advance by him himself."

"Many thanks, and goodbye," said Don Lollò, hurrying away.

Upon his return, toward evening, he found all the farmhands making merry around the inhabited jar. Even the watchdog was taking part in the fun. Not only had Uncle Dima calmed down; he, too, had begun to enjoy his unusual adventure and was laughing with the malicious gaiety that sad people have.

Zirafa made them all move away, and leaned over to look inside the jar.

"Ah! Are you comfortable?"

"Fine. In the cooler,"[4] he replied. "Better off than at home."

"Glad to hear it. Meanwhile I'll have you note that this jar cost me four *onze* new. How much do you think it would be worth now?"

"With me inside?" asked Uncle Dima.

The countryfolk laughed.

"Quiet!" shouted Zirafa. "It's one or the other: either your cement works or it doesn't work; if it doesn't work, you're a swindler; if it does work, the jar, just as it is, must have some value. What value? You judge."

Uncle Dima reflected for a while, then said:

"I'm answering. If you had allowed me to mend it with nothing but cement, the way I wanted, first of all I wouldn't be in here, and the jar would be worth just about the same as before. But sloppily mended with these ugly rivets that I was compelled to put in it from inside here, what value could it have? A third of its original value, more or less."

---

[4] A pun: literally, "in the cool" (that is, out of the heat of the sun); humorously, "in jail."

"A third?" asked Zirafa. "One *onza,* thirty-three?"

"Maybe less, not more."

"All right," said Don Lollò. "Let your words be good, and give me seventeen *lire.*"

"What?" asked Uncle Dima, as if he hadn't understood.

"I will break the jar to let you out," answered Don Lollò, "and you, as the lawyer says, pay me what it's worth: one *onza,* thirty-three."

"I should pay?" sneered Uncle Dima. "You're joking, sir. I'll rot in here."

And, with some difficulty pulling his little tartar-incrusted pipe out of his pocket, he lit it and began smoking, driving the smoke out of the neck of the jar.

Don Lollò began to sulk. This additional possibility, that Uncle Dima would refuse to leave the jar, neither he nor the lawyer had foreseen. And how could things be settled now? He was just about to give the command "The mule!" again, but restrained himself in time, reflecting that it was already evening.

"Oh, is that so?" he said. "You want to take up residence in my jar? You're all witnesses here! He doesn't want to get out, to avoid paying for it; I'm ready to break it! Meanwhile, since he wants to stay there, tomorrow I'll present him with a summons for squatting on my property, because he's preventing me from using the jar!"

First Uncle Dima sent out another mouthful of smoke, then he replied, calmly:

"No, sir. I don't want to prevent you from doing anything. Am I here for my pleasure? Get me out, but I'm not paying a thing! Don't even say it as a joke, sir!"

Don Lollò, in a fit of rage, lifted one foot to give the jar a kick; but he stopped short; instead, he seized it with both hands and shook it vigorously, trembling and shouting to the old man:

"Scoundrel, who did the damage, you or me? And I'm supposed to pay for it? Die of hunger in there! We'll see who wins!"

And he went away, not thinking of the three *lire* he had thrown into the jar that morning. To begin with, it occurred to Uncle Dima to use that money to have a party that evening along with the farmhands, who, having stayed late because of that strange accident, were planning to spend the night in the countryside, outdoors, on the threshing floor. One of them went to make the purchases at a nearby tavern. As it turned out, the moon shone so brightly it seemed like daylight.

At a certain hour Don Lollò, who had gone to bed, was awakened by an infernal racket. Coming out onto a balcony of the farmhouse, he saw on the threshing floor, in the moonlight, a swarm of devils: the drunken farmhands who had linked hands and were dancing around the jar. Uncle Dima, inside, was singing at the top of his voice.

This time Don Lollò could no longer control himself: he dashed over like a maddened bull and, before they had time to ward him off, gave the jar a big push that sent it tumbling down the hillside. Rolling, to the accompaniment of the drunkards' laughter, the jar smashed up against an olive tree.

And Uncle Dima won.

IT'S NOT TO BE TAKEN SERIOUSLY

Perazzetti? No. He was certainly in a class of his own.

He would say things with the utmost seriousness, so that you wouldn't even know it was him, while he looked at his extremely long, curved fingernails, of which he took the most meticulous care.

It's true that then, all of a sudden, for no apparent reason . . . exactly like a duck: he would burst out into certain fits of laughter that were like the quacking of a duck; and he would wallow around in that laughter just like a duck.

Many, many people found in that very laughter the best proof that Perazzetti was crazy. Seeing him writhe with tears in his eyes, his friends would ask him:

"But why?"

And he would reply:

"It's nothing. I can't tell you."

When people saw him laughing like that and refusing to say why, they got disconcerted, they stood there looking like fools and experienced a certain physical irritation, which in the case of the so-called "nervous types" could easily develop into a ferocious rage and an urge to scratch him.

Unable to scratch him, the so-called "nervous types" (and there are so many of them nowadays) would shake their heads furiously and say in reference to Perazzetti:

"He's a lunatic!"

If, instead, Perazzetti had told them the reason for that quacking of his . . . But frequently, Perazzetti couldn't tell them; he honestly couldn't tell them.

He had an extremely active and terrifically capricious imagination, which, when he saw other people, would fly out of control and, without his volition, would arouse in his mind the most outrageous images, flashes of inexpressibly hilarious visions; it would suddenly reveal to him certain hidden analogies, or unexpectedly indicate to

him certain contrasts that were so grotesque and comic that he
would burst out laughing unrestrainedly.

How could he make other people share the instantaneous inter-
play of those fleeting, unpremeditated images?

Perazzetti knew clearly, from his own experience, how different
the basic essence of every man is from the fictitious interpretations
of that essence that each of us offers himself either spontaneously,
or through unconscious self-deceit, out of that need to think ourselves or to be thought different from what we are, either because
we imitate others or because of social necessities and conventions.

He had made a special study of that basic essence of being, and
called it "the cave of the beast," of the primordial beast lurking
inside each of us, beneath all the layers of our consciousness which
have been gradually superimposed on it over the years. A man,
when touched or tickled on this or that layer, would respond with
bows, with smiles, would extend his hand, would say "good day"
and "good evening," might even lend five *lire:* but woe to anyone
who went and poked him down there, in the cave of the beast: out
would come the thief, the impostor, the murderer. It's true that,
after so many centuries of civilization, many people now sheltered
in their cave an animal that was excessively subdued: a pig that said
the rosary, a fox that had lost its tail.

In restaurants, for example, Perazzetti would study the cus-
tomers' controlled impatience. On the outside, good manners; on
the inside, the donkey who wanted his grain immediately. And he
enjoyed himself no end imagining all the species of animals who
had their lair in the caves belonging to the men he was acquainted
with: this man surely had an anteater inside him, and that man a
porcupine and that other man a turkey, and so on.

Often, however, Perazzetti's bursts of laughter had a reason that
I might call more permanent; and, indeed, that reason couldn't be
blurted out, just like that, to everybody; rather, it was to be confided, if at all, very quietly into someone's ear. When thus confided,
I assure you that it inevitably provoked the noisiest outbreak of
laughter. Once he confided it to a friend to whom he was eager to
prove that he wasn't crazy.

I can't tell you the reason out loud; I can only give you some
bare indication of it; try to comprehend it from my hint, because,
if it were told out loud, among other things it might very well seem
to be indecent, and it's not.

Perazzetti was not a vulgar man; on the contrary, he claimed to

have a very high esteem for humanity, for all that it has managed
to accomplish from ancient Greek times to our own day, in spite
of the primordial beast; but Perazzetti was unable to forget the fact
that man, who has been capable of creating so many beautiful
things, is still compelled daily to obey certain intimate and unseemly
natural necessities, which surely do him no credit.

Seeing a poor man, a poor woman in a humble and modest attitude, Perazzetti didn't think about it; but when he saw certain
women giving themselves sentimental airs, certain pompous men
loaded with self-conceit, it was a disaster: immediately, irresistibly
there leaped into his mind the image of those intimate and unseemly natural necessities, which even they definitely had to obey
daily: he saw them in that posture and would burst out laughing
mercilessly.

There was no masculine nobility or feminine beauty that could
escape that disaster in Perazzetti's imagination; in fact, the more
ethereal and idealized a woman's presence seemed to him, the more
a man had put on an air of majesty, all the more did that accursed
image awake within him unexpectedly.

Now, with this in mind, just imagine Perazzetti in love.

And fall in love he did, unlucky man, he fell in love with extraordinary ease! He no longer thought about anything, he was no
longer himself, the moment he was in love; he immediately became
another man, became that Perazzetti which others wished him to
be, the sort of man that not only the woman into whose hands he
had fallen wanted to mold him into, but also the sort of man that
the future fathers-in-law, future brothers-in-law and even the
friends of the bride's family wanted to mold him into.

He had been engaged at least twenty or so times. And he would
make you split your sides laughing when he described all the different Perazzettis he had been, each one dumber and more idiotic
than the last: the one with the mother-in-law's parrot, the one with
the young sister-in-law's interest in the stars, the one with some
friend or other's stringbeans.

Whenever the heat of passion, which had brought him into a
state of fusion, so to speak, began to abate, and he gradually began
to gell into his customary shape and recover self-consciousness, at
first he felt amazement and alarm at observing the shape they had
given him, the role they had made him play, the state of idiocy to
which they had reduced him; then, as he looked at his fiancée, as

he looked at the mother-in-law, as he looked at the father-in-law, the terrible laughter would start all over again, and he had to flee—there was no other way—he had to flee.

But the trouble was that they were no longer willing to let him escape. He was an excellent young man, Perazzetti, well-to-do, extremely likable.

If the dramas enacted in those twenty or more engagements were assembled in a book as narrated by him, they would be among the most amusing reading materials of our generation. But what would be laughs for the reader were unfortunately tears, real tears for poor Perazzetti, fits of rage and of anguish, and despair.

Each time he promised and swore to himself that he wouldn't relapse; he resolved to think up some heroic cure that would prevent him from falling in love again. But no! He would relapse shortly afterward, and always worse than before.

Finally, one day the news that he had married burst like a bomb. And he had married none other than . . . But no, nobody wanted to believe it! Perazzetti had done all sorts of crazy things; but that he could go that far, to the point of tying himself for the rest of his life to a woman like that . . .

Tying himself? When one of his many friends, visiting him at home, came out with that expression, it was a wonder that Perazzetti didn't kill him.

"Tie myself? What do you mean, tie myself? Why is it tying myself? You're all stupid, foolish idiots! Tie myself? Who said so? Do I look tied to you? Come with me, come in here . . . This is my regular bed, isn't it? Does it look like a double bed? Hey, Cecchino! Cecchino!"

Cecchino was his trusty old servant.

"Tell me, Cecchino. Do I come here every night to sleep, alone?"

"Yes, sir, alone."

"Every night?"

"Every night."

"Where do I eat?"

"In that room."

"With whom do I eat?"

"All alone."

"Do you prepare my food?"

"Yes, sir."

"And am I still the same Celestino?"

"Still the same, sir."

Sending away the servant, after that interrogation, Perazzetti concluded, opening his arms:

"And so . . . "

"So it's not true?" the other asked.

"Of course, it's true! True as can be! Absolutely true!" answered Perazzetti. "I married her! I married her in church and at the registry office! But what does that mean? You think it's something serious?"

"No, just the opposite, totally ridiculous."

"Well, there you have it!" Perazzetti concluded once more. "Get out of my way! You've all finished laughing behind my back! You pictured me dead, didn't you? With a noose always around my neck! Enough, enough, friends! Now I've freed myself for good! All it took was that last storm, from which I escaped alive by a miracle . . . "

The last storm to which Perazzetti alluded was his engagement to the daughter of the head of a division at the finance ministry, Commendatore[1] Vico Lamanna; and Perazzetti was perfectly right in saying that he had escaped it alive by a miracle. He had had to fight a sword duel with the woman's brother, Lino Lamanna, an excellent swordsman; and because he was a very good friend of Lino's and felt he had nothing, absolutely nothing against him, he had let himself be handsomely skewered like a chicken.

It seemed as if this time—and anyone would have called it a sure thing —the wedding was definitely going to take place. Miss Elly Lamanna, brought up in English fashion—as could be seen even from her name—forthright, frank, solid, well-poised (read: American-style shoes), had doubtless succeeded in avoiding that usual disaster in Perazzetti's imagination. Yes, a bit of laughter had escaped him when looking at his father-in-law the Commendatore, who even with him remained on his high horse and would sometimes speak to him with that pomade-like stickiness of his . . . But enough of that. He had courteously confided to his fiancée the reason for those bursts of laughter; she had laughed over it herself; and when that reef had been passed, Perazzetti too believed that this time he would finally reach the safe harbor of matrimony (so to speak). The mother-in-law was a kind old lady, modest and taci-

---

[1] Member of an order of chivalry.

turn, and Lino, the brother, seemed perfectly suited to see eye to eye with him in every possible way.

Indeed, from the first day of the engagement, Perazzetti and Lino Lamanna became two inseparable companions. You might say that Perazzetti spent more time with his future brother-in-law than with his fiancée: outings, hunting trips, horseback rides together, together on the Tiber at the boating club.

He could imagine anything, poor Perazzetti, except that this time the disaster was to strike him because of his excessive closeness to his future brother-in-law, on account of another quirk of his morbid and ludicrous imagination.

At a certain point, he began to discover in his fiancée a disturbing resemblance to her brother.

It was at Livorno, at the seaside, where he had naturally gone with the Lamannas.

Perazzetti had seen Lino in a sporting jersey plenty of times when rowing; now he saw his fiancée in a bathing suit. It should be noted that Lino really did look ever so slightly feminine, in the hips.

What was the effect on Perazzetti when he discovered that resemblance? He broke out into a cold sweat, he began to feel an unconquerable repulsion at the thought of initiating marital intimacies with Elly Lamanna, who looked so much like her brother. He suddenly pictured those intimacies as something monstrous, almost unnatural, now that he saw the brother when looking at the fiancée; and he writhed at the slightest caress she gave him, seeing himself looked at by eyes now provocative and inciting, now languishing in the promise of a longed-for sensual pleasure.

But, meanwhile, could Perazzetti shout to her:

"Oh, for God's sake, quit it! Let's call it off! I can be very good friends with Lino, because I don't have to marry him; but I can no longer marry *you*, because it would be like marrying your brother."

The torture that Perazzetti suffered this time was far greater than all those he had suffered in the past. It ended up with that sword thrust, which by a miracle failed to send him to the next world.

And as soon as the wound had healed, he hit upon the heroic cure that was to bar the way to matrimony to him for good.

"But how," I hear you ask, "by getting married?"

Of course! Maddalena: the one with the dog; by marrying Maddalena, of course, that poor nitwit that you could see every night on the street, decked out in certain hideous hats loaded down with fluttering greenery, pulled along by a black poodle that never gave her the time to finish those "killing" little laughs of hers, directed at policemen, young boys still wet behind the ears, and soldiers, because it was in such a hurry—damned dog—to get who knows where, to who knows what faraway dark corner . . .

He married her in church and at the registry office; he took her off the street; he gave her an allowance of two *lire* a day and shipped her off far away, into the country.

His friends—as you can imagine—gave him no peace for quite some time. But Perazzetti had now calmly returned to his habit of saying things with the utmost seriousness, so that you wouldn't even know it was him, while looking at his nails.

"Yes," he would say. "I married her. But it's nothing serious. As for sleeping, I sleep alone, at home; as for eating, I eat alone, at home; I don't see her; she doesn't bother me at all . . . You say, what about my name? Yes: I gave her my name. But, gentlemen, what's a name? It's not to be taken seriously."

Strictly speaking, nothing was serious to Perazzetti. Everything depends on the importance you attach to things. If you attach importance to the most ridiculous thing, it can become deadly serious, and vice versa, the most serious matter can become altogether ridiculous. Is there anything more serious than death? And yet, for those many people who attach no importance to it . . .

All right; but his friends wanted to see him a few days later. Who knows how he would regret it!

"No kidding!" Perazzetti would answer. "Of course I'll regret it! I'm already beginning to regret it . . . "

When he came out with that sally, his friends would begin to cry out:

"Ah! You see?"

"But, you fools," Perazzetti would retort, "at the exact moment I truly regret it, I'll reap the benefit of my cure, because that will mean I've fallen in love again, to the point of committing the most vulgar of bestial acts: that of taking a wife."

Chorus of voices:

"But you've already taken one!"

Perazzetti:

"That one? Go on, now! That one's not to be taken seriously."

Conclusion:

Perazzetti had gotten married to protect himself from the danger of taking a wife.

THINK IT OVER, GIACOMINO!

For three days Professor[1] Agostino Toti hasn't had at home that peace, that laughter to which he thinks he is by now entitled.

Yes, he's about seventy, and you couldn't even say that he was a fine-looking old man: on the short side, with a big bald head, no neck, an outsize torso on two skinny legs like a bird's . . .

Professor Toti is well aware of this, and doesn't delude himself in the least, therefore, into thinking that Maddalena, his pretty little wife, who is not yet twenty-six, can love him for his own sake.

It's true that she was poor when he took her and that he improved her station in life: the daughter of a janitor in the high school, she became the wife of a permanent-staff teacher of natural sciences, with a claim to the maximum pension in a few months now; not only that, but also wealthy for the last two years thanks to an unexpected piece of good luck, truly like manna from heaven: an inheritance of nearly two hundred thousand *lire*, from a brother who had emigrated to Romania long ago and had died there a bachelor.

And yet, even with all that, Professor Toti wouldn't think he had a right to peace and laughter. He's a philosopher: he knows that all this wouldn't be enough for a young, pretty wife.

If his inheritance had arrived before the wedding, he might possibly have been able to ask Maddalena to have a little patience, that is, to wait for his death, not far off now, in order to be compensated for the sacrifice of having married an old man. But those two hundred thousand *lire* had come too late, two years after the wedding, when already . . . when Professor Toti had already philosophically realized that the small pension alone that he would leave her one day couldn't suffice to repay his wife for her sacrifice.

Having already made all those concessions, Professor Toti thinks he is more right than ever in claiming peace and laughter now, with the addition of that respectable inheritance. All the more so

---

[1] Toti is a *professore ordinario* in a *liceo*. A *liceo* corresponds more or less to an American high school, but even high-school teachers are addressed as "Professore" in Italy. At a university a *professore ordinario* would be a "full professor"; here it has been rendered as "permanent-staff teacher."

because—being a truly wise and decent man—he wasn't satisfied with benefiting his wife, but also decided to benefit . . . yes, him, his good Giacomino, formerly one of his best students at the high school, a shy, honest, very courteous young man, handsome as a cherub.

Yes, yes—old Professor Agostino Toti has done everything, has thought of everything, philosophically. Giacomino Pugliese had been unemployed, and his idleness was troubling him and depressing him; all right, he, Professor Toti, had found him a job in the Farmers' Bank, where he deposited the two hundred thousand *lire* he had inherited.

There's a child in the house, too, now, a little angel of two and a half, to whom he has become entirely devoted, like a loving slave. Every day he can't wait for the lessons at the high school to be over, so he can run home and humor his little tyrant's slightest whim. To tell the truth, after the inheritance he could have retired, giving up that maximum pension, so that he could spend all his time with the child. But no! It would have been a sin! Inasmuch as it exists, he wants to bear that yoke of his, which he has always found so burdensome, to the very end! After all, he took a wife for that very reason, just so someone could benefit from what had been a torment to him all his life!

Marrying with this single purpose, to benefit a poor young woman, he has loved his wife solely with a quasi-paternal affection. And he started loving her more paternally than ever from the time the child was born, the child by whom he would almost prefer to be called grandfather rather than daddy. This unwitting lie on the pure little lips of the ignorant child hurts him; he feels that even his love for him suffers from it. But what's to be done? He *must* receive with a kiss that name coming from Ninì's sweet little mouth, that "daddy" which gets a laugh from all the spiteful people who are unable to understand his loving feelings for that innocent creature, his happiness over the good that he has done and continues to do for a woman, a worthy young man, the little one, and himself as well—of course!—himself as well—the happiness of living these last years in cheerful, pleasant company, walking on the edge of the grave with a little angel holding his hand.

Let them laugh, let all the spiteful people laugh at him! What does that matter to him? He is happy.

But for three days . . .

What can have happened? His wife's eyes are swollen and red from crying; she says she has a bad headache; she doesn't want to leave her room.

"Ah, youth! . . . youth! . . ." Professor Toti sighs, shaking his head with a sad, sly smile in his eyes and on his lips. "Some cloud . . . some little thunderstorm . . ."

And with Ninì he wanders around the house, troubled, nervous, also a little irritated, because . . . no, he really doesn't deserve such treatment from his wife and from Giacomino. Young people don't count the days: they have so many still ahead of them . . . But for a poor old man the loss of a day is serious! And it's been three now that his wife has been leaving him alone in the house this way, like a fly without a head, and no longer treating him to those little airs and songs sung in her clear, impassioned little voice, and no longer lavishing those cares on him to which he is now accustomed.

Ninì, too, is as serious as can be, as if he understands that his Mommy's mind is too occupied to pay attention to him. The Professor takes him along from one room to the other, and has practically no need to stoop down to give him his hand, he's so small himself; he leads him in front of the piano, presses down a few keys here and there, snorts, yawns, then sits down, gives Ninì a ride on his knees for a while, then stands up again: he's on pins and needles. Five or six times he has tried to force his little wife to speak.

"Bad, eh? You're really feeling bad?"

Little Maddalena persists in not wanting to tell him anything; she weeps; she asks him to close the balcony shutters and take Ninì to another room: she wants to be alone in the dark.

"Your head, eh?"

Poor thing, her head aches so . . . Ah, the quarrel must have been really a major one!

Professor Toti moves on to the kitchen and tries to start a conversation with the young maid, to get some information out of her; but he beats around the bush, because he knows that the maid is hostile to him; she speaks ill of him, outside the house, like all the rest, and criticizes him. He fails to learn anything, even from the maid.

And then Professor Toti makes a heroic resolution: he takes Ninì to his mother and asks her to dress him up nicely.

"Why?" she asks.

"I'm taking him for a little walk," he replies. "Today is a holiday . . . He's bored here, poor kid!"

His mother is unwilling. She knows that evil-minded people laugh when they see the old Professor walking hand in hand with the little one; she knows that one insolent scoundrel went so far as to say to him: "My, how your son resembles you, Professor!"

But Professor Toti insists.

"No, for a walk, for a walk . . . "

And with the child he goes to Giacomino Pugliese's house.

Giacomino lives together with a sister of marriageable age who has been a mother to him. Unaware of the reason for the kindnesses showered on her brother, Miss Agata was at first very grateful to Professor Toti; now, instead—being extremely religious—she puts him on a par with the devil, neither more nor less, because he has led her Giacomino into mortal sin.

Professor Toti has to wait in front of the door with the little one for quite some time after ringing the bell. Miss Agata came to look through the peephole and fled. No doubt she went to inform her brother of the visit, and now she'll come back and say that Giacomino isn't home.

Here she is. Dressed in black, with a waxen complexion, thin as a stick, sullen, as soon as the door is open she attacks the Professor, all aquiver.

"How's this? . . . Excuse me . . . Now you're coming to see him in his own house, too? . . . And what's this I see? With the child, too? You brought the child, too?"

Professor Toti wasn't expecting this kind of reception; he's dumbfounded; he looks at Miss Agata, looks at the little one, smiles, stammers:

"Wh. . . why? . . . What's wrong? . . . Can't I . . . can't . . . can't I come to . . . "

"He's not in!" she hurriedly resumes, in her arid, harsh manner. "Giacomino's not in."

"All right," says Professor Toti, bowing his head. "But you, Miss . . . forgive me . . . you treat me in a fashion that . . . I don't know! I don't think I've dealt with either your brother or you . . . "

"Now, Professor," Miss Agata interrupts him, somewhat appeased. "Believe me, we're . . . we're extremely grateful to you, but even *you* ought to understand . . . "

Professor Toti half-closes his eyes, smiles again, raises one hand

and then touches his chest several times with his fingertips to indicate that, when it comes to understanding, he's the one for the job.

"I'm old, Miss," he says, "and I do understand . . . I understand so many things! And look, first and foremost, I understand this: that it's necessary to let certain angers evaporate and, when misunderstandings arise, the best thing is to clarify matters . . . to clarify them, Miss, clarify them frankly, without subterfuges, without getting heated up . . . Don't you agree?"

"Of course I do . . . ," Miss Agata acknowledges, at least in the abstract.

"And so," resumes Professor Toti, "let me in and call Giacomino for me."

"But I tell you he's not in!"

"You see? No. You mustn't tell me he's not in. Giacomino is at home, and you must call him for me. We'll clarify everything calmly . . . tell him that: calmly! I'm old and I understand everything, because I was also young once, Miss. Calmly, tell him that. Let me in."

Ushered into the humble parlor, Professor Toti sits down with Ninì between his knees, resigned to waiting a long time here, too, while Giacomino's sister is persuading him to come.

"No, here, Ninì . . . that's a good boy!" he says from time to time to the child, who would like to go over to a shelf on which some porcelain knickknacks are sparkling; and meanwhile he racks his brains wondering what the devil could have happened in his house that was so serious, without his having noticed it at all. Little Maddalena is so good-natured! What wrong could she have committed to cause such a fierce and strong resentment, here, even in Giacomino's sister?

Professor Toti, who up to now has thought it was a passing spat, is starting to get worried and seriously alarmed.

Ah, here is Giacomino finally! God, what an angry face! What a ruffled manner! What's this? Oh, no, not that! He coldly shuns the child, who has run to meet him with his little hands outstretched, crying:

"'Giamì! Giamì!'"

"Giacomino!" Professor Toti, who is hurt, exclaims with severity.

"What do you have to say to me, Professor?" Giacomino quickly asks him, avoiding looking him in the eye. "I'm unwell . . . I was in bed . . . I'm in no shape to talk or even bear the sight of anybody . . . "

"But the child?!"

"There," Giacomino says; and he stoops down to kiss Ninì.

"You're not well?" Professor Toti resumes, somewhat comforted by that kiss. "I thought as much. And that's why I came. Your head, eh? Sit down, sit down . . . Let's have a talk. Here, Ninì . . . You hear? 'Giamì' is 'sick.' Yes, dear, 'sick' . . . here, poor 'Giamì' . . . Be good; we're leaving right away. I meant to ask you," he adds, addressing Giacomino, "whether the director of the Farmers' Bank told you anything."

"No, why?" says Giacomino, becoming even more perturbed.

"Because I spoke to him yesterday," says Professor Toti with a mysterious little smile. "Your salary isn't all that big, son. And you know that a word from me . . . "

Giacomino Pugliese writhes on his chair and clenches his fists till he sinks his nails into the palms of his hands.

"Professor, I thank you," he says, "but do me the favor, the very great favor, of no longer troubling yourself over me, won't you?"

"Oh, really?" answers Professor Toti with that little smile still on his lips. "Good man! We no longer need anybody, eh? But what if I wanted to do it for my own pleasure? My good man, if I'm not to take care of you any more, whom do you want me to take of? I'm old, Giacomino! And old people—assuming they're not selfish!—old people like to see deserving youngsters like you get ahead in life with their help; and they get enjoyment out of the youngsters' happiness, their hopes, the position they gradually assume in society. Now, with regard to you, I . . . come now, you know it . . . I look on you as a son . . . What's wrong? You're crying?"

Indeed, Giacomino has hidden his face in his hands and is shaken as if by an attack of weeping that he'd like to hold back.

Ninì looks at him in dismay, then, addressing the Professor, says: "'Giamì,' sick . . . "

The Professor gets up and starts to put a hand on Giacomino's shoulder; but the young man leaps to his feet as if repelled at the thought, shows his face, which is distorted as if by a sudden fierce resolution, and shouts at him in exasperation:

"Don't come near me! Professor, go away, I beg of you, go away! You're making me suffer the torments of hell! I don't deserve this affection of yours and I don't want it, I don't want it . . . For heaven's sake, go away, take away the child and forget that I exist!"

Professor Toti stands there amazed; he asks:

"But why?"

"I'll tell you right away!" Giacomino answers. "I'm engaged, Professor! Understand? I'm engaged!"

Professor Toti staggers, as if hit on the head with a club; he raises his hands; stammers:

"You? En. . . engaged?"

"Yes, sir," says Giacomino. "And so, enough . . . enough for always! You'll understand that I can no longer . . . see you here . . . "

"You're throwing me out?" Professor Toti asks, almost tonelessly.

"No!" Giacomino hurriedly replies, in his sorrow. "But it would be good for you . . . for you to go away, Professor . . . "

Go away? The professor plumps down on a chair. His legs seem to have been knocked out from under him. He takes his head in his hands and moans:

"Oh, God! Ah, what a catastrophe! And so this was the reason? What shall I do? What shall I do? But when? How? Without saying a thing? To whom are you engaged?"

"Here, Professor . . . for some time," says Giacomino. "To a poor orphan like myself . . . a friend of my sister's . . . "

Professor Toti looks at him numbly, with his eyes dulled, his mouth open, and can't summon up his voice to go on speaking.

"And . . . and . . . and everything is abandoned . . . like this . . . and . . . and no more thought is given to . . . to anything . . . no more . . . no more account is taken of anything . . . "

Giacomino feels that he is being reproached with ingratitude, and he protests, gloomily:

"Just a moment! You wanted me to be a slave?"

"I . . . a slave?" Professor Toti now bursts out, with a crack in his voice. "I? And you can say that? I, who made you master in my own house? Ah, this, yes, this is true ingratitude! And was it perhaps for my sake that I benefited you? What did I get out of it, except the mockery of all the fools who can't understand my feelings? And so you don't understand them, not even you have understood them, the feelings of this poor old man who is about to depart from the scene and who was calmly contented to leave everything arranged, a little family that was doing well, in comfortable circumstances . . . happy? I'm seventy years old; tomorrow I'll be gone, Giacomino! You've lost your mind, son! I'm leaving you two everything, here . . . What are you still looking for? I don't know yet, I don't want to know, who your fiancée is; I'm sure she's a respectable young woman, because *you* are so fine . . . ; but just think that . . . just think that . . . it isn't possible for you to have found anything better, Giacomino, from any point of view . . . I don't mean merely because of the guaranteed financial comfort . . . But you already have your own little family, of which I'm the only super-fluous member, and that not for long . . . and I don't count at all . . . What bother do I give you two? I'm like your father . . . If you like, I can even . . . for your peace of mind . . . But tell me how it came about. What happened? How did your head turn so suddenly? Tell me! Tell me . . . "

And Professor Toti goes over to Giacomino and wants to take him by the arm and shake it; but Giacomino tenses up, as if shuddering, and wards him off.

"Professor!" he shouts. "How is it that you don't understand, that you don't realize that all this kindness of yours . . . "

"Well?"

"Let me be! Don't make me say it! How is it you don't understand that certain things can be done only clandestinely, and are no longer possible in the full light of the day, with you knowing about them, with all the people laughing over them?"

"Oh, it's on account of the people?" exclaims the Professor. "And you . . . "

"Let me be!" Giacomino repeats, at the peak of his excitement, waving his arms in the air. "Look! There are so many other young men in need of assistance, Professor!"

Toti feels hurt to the bottom of his heart by these words, which are a horrible, unjust insult to his wife; he turns pale, he becomes livid, and, trembling all over, he says:

"Little Maddalena is young, but she's respectable, damn it! And you know it! Maddalena may die of this . . . because her pain is here, here, in the heart . . . Where do you think it is? It's here, it's here, you ingrate! Ah, now you're insulting her, on top of every-thing else? And you're not ashamed? And you don't feel any re-morse on my account? You have the nerve to say that to my face? You? You think she can change hands like that, from one man to another, and think nothing of it? The mother of this little one? But what are you saying? How can you talk that way?"

Giacomino looks at him, shocked and astounded.

"I?" he says. "But, Professor, forgive me, it's actually *you*,

you—how can *you* talk like that? Are you serious? What am I? Am I the husband of your wife? And what are you? My father-in-law? Come, now!"

Professor Toti clasps both hands to his mouth, presses his eyes shut, shakes his head and breaks out into despairing tears. Then Ninì, too, starts to cry. The Professor hears him, runs to him, embraces him.

"Ah, my poor Ninì . . . oh, what a disaster, my Ninì, what a catastrophe! And what will become of your Mommy now? And what will become of you, my Ninì, with a little mother like yours, inexperienced, with no one to guide her . . . ? Oh, what hell!"

He lifts his head, and, looking at Giacomino through his tears:

"I'm crying," he says, "because the remorse is mine. I protected you, I took you into my home, I always spoke so well of you to her, I . . . I removed all the scruples she had about loving you . . . and now that she was safely in love with you . . . the mother of this little one . . . you . . . "

He breaks off and, sternly, resolutely, nervously:

"Watch out, Giacomino!" he says. "I'm capable of showing up at your fiancée's house hand in hand with this little one!"

Giacomino, in a cold sweat even though on hot coals from hearing him speak and cry like that, at that threat puts his hands together, moves in front of him and beseeches him:

"Professor, Professor, do you really want to cover yourself with ridicule?"

"With ridicule?" shouts the Professor. "And what difference do you want that to make to me, when I see the destruction of a poor woman, your destruction, the destruction of an innocent baby? Come, come, we're going, come now, Ninì, we're going!"

Giacomino comes up to him.

"Professor, you won't do that!"

"I *will* do it!" Professor Toti shouts to him with a resolute expression. "And to prevent that marriage of yours, I'm even capable of having you thrown out of the bank! I give you three days' time."

And, turning around on the threshold, holding the little one by the hand:

"Think it over, Giacomino! Think it over!"

A CHARACTER'S TRAGEDY

I persist in my old habit of giving audience every Sunday morning to the characters of my future short stories.

Three hours, from seven to ten.

I almost always find myself in bad company.

I don't know why, but usually those who attend my audiences are the most discontented people in the world, either suffering from strange maladies, or entangled in the most singular situations, people with whom it's really a torment to deal.

I listen to them all with infinite forbearing; I take down each one's name and circumstances; I take into account their feelings and aspirations; I question them courteously and make the greatest possible effort to satisfy them; that is, to accept them in my own mind and in my writings just as they see themselves in their own mind as individuals.

But I must also add that, by my nature and to my misfortune, I myself am not easily pleased. Patience, courtesy—yes, I have those; but I don't like being hoodwinked. And it's my custom to get to the bottom of each matter, making a long, detailed investigation.

Now, it's often the case that at certain questions I pose they jib, they take umbrage, they resist furiously, because they think that I'm getting enjoyment out of demolishing the serious front with which they come to me.

"What does that have to do with anything?"

Using my patience and my courtesy, I do my best to make them see and perceive that my question was perfectly à propos, because it's easy for anyone to *wish* to be one kind of person or another; the real question is whether we *can* be the way we want to be. When the power to do so is lacking, the wish must necessarily appear ridiculous and vain.

They can't be convinced of this.

And then, being basically good-hearted, I'm sorry for them. But is it ever possible to feel sorry for certain misfortunes unless you can laugh at them at the same time?

Well, the characters of my stories go around spreading the word everywhere that I am an extremely cruel and merciless writer. It would take a critic possessed of good will to make people see how much sympathy underlies that laughter.

But where are the critics possessed of good will nowadays?

It should be noted that some characters at these audiences leap ahead of the others and make their presence felt with such self-importance that I sometimes find myself compelled to let them enter life out of turn, right on the spot.

A number of them later bitterly regret this furore of theirs and implore me to patch up whatever defect each one has. But I yell at them, saying that now they must atone for their original sin and wait until there is no longer such a big crowd around me and I have the time and the means to get back to them.

Among those who remain behind waiting, feeling overwhelmed, some sigh, some grow sullen, some get tired and go off to knock at some other writer's door. Not seldom I have happened to find in the stories of several colleagues of mine certain characters that had called on me first; just as I have also happened to recognize certain others, who, dissatisfied with the way I had treated them, decided to try and cut a better figure elsewhere.

I don't complain of this, because usually two or three come to see me every week, joining the far from tiny number of those waiting. And often there is such a mob that I have to give my attention to more than one at the same time. Unless, at some point, my mind becomes so distracted and bewildered that it rejects that double or triple nurturing and shouts in its exasperation: "Either one at a time, quietly and calmly, or all three of you can get lost!"

I always remember how meekly one poor old man awaited his turn, after coming a long way to see me: a certain composer named Icilio Saporini, who had emigrated to America in 1849 after the fall of the Roman Republic because he had set a patriotic hymn to music, and had come back to Italy to die forty-five years later, aged almost eighty. Ceremonious, with a tiny voice like a mosquito's, he would let everyone else get ahead of him. And finally, one day when I was still recovering from a long illness, I saw him come into my room, humble as can be, with a timid little smile on his lips:

"If I may . . . If it isn't any trouble . . . "

Of course, dear old man! He had chosen the most opportune moment. And I had him die just as fast as possible in a little story titled "Old Music."[1]

*

---

[1] "Musica vecchia," first published in 1910.

This past Sunday I went into my study, for the audience, a little later than usual.

A long novel that had been sent to me as a gift and had been waiting over a month for me to read it kept me up till three in the morning because of the many reflections aroused in me by one of its characters, the only living one among a crowd of empty shadows.

His role was that of an unfortunate man, a certain Dr. Fileno, who thought he had found the most effective cure for every kind of ailment, an infallible prescription for consoling himself and all men for every public or private calamity.

To tell the truth, rather than a cure or a prescription, this discovery of Dr. Fileno's was a method, which consisted of reading history books from morning till night and of looking on the present as history, too—that is, as something already very remote in time. And with this method he had been cured of all his ills, he had freed himself from every sorrow and every annoyance, and had found peace without the necessity of dying: an austere, serene peace, permeated with that certain sadness without regret which the cemeteries on the earth's surface would still retain even after all the people on earth had died out.

Dr. Fileno hadn't even the slightest thought of deriving lessons from the past for the present, because he knew it would be a waste of time and a game for fools. History is an idealized amalgam of elements gathered together in accordance with the nature, likes, dislikes, aspirations and opinions of historians. How, then, can this idealized amalgam be applied to living, effective reality, in which the elements are still separate and scattered? Nor, similarly, did he have any thought of deriving from the present any norms or predictions for the future. In fact, Dr. Fileno did just the opposite. In his mind he placed himself in the future in order to look back at the present, which he viewed as the past.

For example, a few days earlier a daughter of his had died. A friend had come to see him to condole with him over his misfortune. Well, he had found him as consoled already as if that daughter had died a hundred years before.

He had just taken that misfortune of his, while it was still recent and painful, and had distanced it in time, had relegated it to, and filed it away in, the past.

But you had to see from what a height and with how much dignity he spoke about it!

In short, Dr. Fileno had made a sort of telescope for himself out of that method of his. He would open it, but now not with the intention of looking toward the future, where he knew he would see nothing. He convinced his mind that it should be contented to look through the larger lens, which was pointed at the future, toward the smaller one, which was pointed at the present. And so his mind looked through the "wrong" end of the telescope, and immediately the present became small and very distant.

Dr. Fileno had been looking forward for several years to writing a book that would certainly create a stir. And, in fact, the title of the book was *The Philosophy of Distance*.

While reading the novel it had seemed evident to me that the author, exclusively concerned with artificially weaving one of the most well-worn plots, had been unable to become fully aware of this character, who, containing within himself alone the germ of a true and real creation, had succeeded to some extent in taking over from the author and, for a large part of the book, in standing out in powerful and extraordinary relief against the extremely humdrum events being narrated and performed; then, suddenly denatured, he had allowed himself to be molded and adapted to the exigencies of a false and foolish conclusion.

I had remained for some time, in the silence of the night, with the image of this character before my eyes, giving my imagination free rein. Damn it all, there was enough material in him to produce a masterpiece! If the author hadn't neglected and disregarded him so undeservingly, if he had made him the center of the narrative, all those artificial elements he had had recourse to would also have been transformed, would suddenly have taken on life. And a great sorrow and a great vexation had seized upon me for the sake of that miserably failed life.

Coming into my study late, I found it more crowded than usual. It was disorganized, a muddle. That Dr. Fileno had thrust himself into the midst of my waiting characters, who, angry and irritated, had jumped on him and were trying to drive him away, to pull him back.

"Hey!" I yelled. "Ladies and gentlemen, is this any way to behave? Dr. Fileno, I've already wasted too much time on you, you know! You don't belong to me. Let me now listen to my characters in peace and quiet, and go away. You surely understand that they are right in looking on you and treating you as an intruder and disturber of the peace. Go away!"

Such an intense, despairing anguish was portrayed in Dr. Fileno's face that suddenly all those others, those characters of mine who were still in the act of restraining him, turned pale with mortification and drew back.

"Don't throw me out, for heaven's sake don't throw me out! Grant me just five minutes' audience, and let me persuade you, I beg of you!"

Perplexed and yet filled with pity, I asked him:

"But persuade me about what? I am fully persuaded that you, dear Doctor, deserved to fall into better hands. What do you want me to do for you? I have already lamented your fate sufficiently; now I condole with you personally, and that's the end of it."

"The end of it? No, by God!" exclaimed Dr. Fileno with a shudder of indignation all over his body. "You say that because I'm not one of yours! Believe me, if you showed nonchalance or contempt, it would be much less cruel than this passive pity, unworthy of an artist, if you allow me to say so! No one is in a better position than you to know that we are living beings, more alive than those who breathe and wear clothes; perhaps less real, but truer! There are so many ways of coming to life, sir; and you know very well that nature makes use of the human imagination as a tool for pursuing its work of creation. And anyone who is born thanks to this creative activity which has its seat in the human spirit is ordained by nature for a life that is higher than the life of those born from the mortal womb of a woman. Whoever is born as a character, whoever has the good fortune to be born as a living character, can even thumb his nose at death. He will no longer die! The man will die, the writer who was the natural instrument of his creation; but the creature will no longer die! And in order to live eternally, he hasn't the slightest need of extraordinary gifts or prodigious feats. Tell me, who was Sancho Panza? Tell me, who was Don Abbondio?[2] And yet they live eternally because—as living germs—they had the good fortune to find a fertile womb, an imagination that was able to raise and nourish them.

"Yes, yes, dear Doctor: all that is quite so," I said. "I agree entirely. But, forgive me, I don't yet see what you want of *me*."

"No? You really don't?" said Dr. Fileno. "Have I perhaps come to the wrong place? Have I by chance landed on the world of the Moon? What kind of writer are you? So you seriously don't under-

---

[2] A character in *I promessi sposi* (The Betrothed), the great early nineteenth-century novel by Alessandro Manzoni.

stand the horror of my tragedy? To have the inestimable privilege of being born as a character, now of all times, when material life is so beset with tawdry difficulties which create obstacles for, denature and impoverish every existence; to have the privilege of being born as a living character, and therefore, petty as I may be, ordained for immortality and—just think of it!—to fall into those hands, to be condemned to perish unjustly, to suffocate in that artificial world in which I can't draw a free breath or take one step, because it's all made up, fake, contrived, a sham! Words and paper! Paper and words! If a man finds himself entangled in circumstances of living to which he is physically or mentally unable to adapt, he can escape, run away; but a poor character can't: he's stuck there, nailed to an endless martyrdom! Air! Air! Life! Just look . . . 'Fileno' . . . He gave me the name 'Fileno' . . . Do you seriously think that I can be called Fileno? The imbecile, the imbecile! He couldn't even give me a proper name! I, Fileno! And then, I, I, the author of *The Philosophy of Distance*, I of all people had to end up in that wretched way in order to unravel that whole stupid tangle of incidents! Did *I* really have to marry her, that ninny Graziella, instead of the notary Negroni? Don't give me that! These are crimes, my good man, crimes that should be atoned for with tears of blood! Now, what will happen instead? Nothing. Silence. Or perhaps some bad reviews in two or three minor newspapers. Maybe some critic will exclaim: "That poor Fileno, what a shame! *He* really was a good character." And that will be the end of the whole thing. Condemned to death—I, the author of *The Philosophy of Distance*, which that imbecile didn't even see his way to have me publish at my own expense! Otherwise, tell me, how could I have married that ninny Graziella after that? Oh, don't even let me think about it! Come, come, get to work, get to work, my dear sir! Redeem me, at once, at once! You, who have clearly understood all the life there is in me, let me live!"

On hearing this proposal, furiously flung out as the conclusion to this very lengthy outburst, I was stunned for a while and just stared at Dr. Fileno's face.

"Do you have qualms about it?" he asked, growing disturbed. "Do you have any qualms? It's perfectly legitimate, you know! It's your sacrosanct right to take me over and give me the life that that imbecile was unable to give me! It's your right and mine, understand?"

"It may be your right, dear Doctor," I replied, "and it may even be legitimate, as you believe; but I just don't do things like that. There's no use your insisting. I don't do that. Try applying to somebody else."

"And to whom would you have me apply, if you . . . "

"I don't know! Try. Maybe you won't have much trouble finding someone who is perfectly convinced of the legitimacy of that right. Or else there's this: listen a moment, dear Dr. Fileno. Yes or no, are you really the author of *The Philosophy of Distance?*"

"Of course!" said Dr. Fileno, taking a step backward and placing both hands on his chest. "Do you dare doubt it? I understand, I understand! As usual, it's the fault of that man who murdered me! He just barely, in summary, in passing, gave an idea of my theories, not even remotely imagining all the benefit that could be derived from that discovery of mine of looking through the wrong end of the telescope!"

I put out my hands to stop him, smiling and saying:

"All right . . . all right . . . but, tell me, what about *you?*"

"I? Where do *I* come in?"

"You're complaining about your author; but, my dear Doctor, were *you* really able to derive benefit from your theory? There, that's exactly what I wanted to say to you. Let me speak. If you seriously believe, as I do, in the efficacy of your philosophy, why don't you apply a little of it to your own case? Here you are, seeking out from among us a writer who will make you immortal. But look at us all, one by one, putting me at the very end of the line, naturally. And, along with us, look through your celebrated wrong-end-of-the-telescope at the most notable events, the most burning questions and the most admirable accomplishments of our day. My dear Doctor, I'm very much afraid that you will no longer see anything or anybody. And so, come now, cheer up or, rather, resign yourself, and let me listen to my own poor characters, who may be a bad lot and may be peevish, but at least don't have your wild ambition."

A PRANCING HORSE

The moment the head groom left, cursing more than usual, Fofo turned toward Blackie, his newly arrived mangermate, and sighed:

"I get it! Saddlecloths, tassels and plumes. You're off to a good start, fellow! It's a first-class one today."

Blackie turned his head in the other direction. He didn't snort, because he was a well-brought-up horse. But he didn't want to confide in that Fofo.

He came from a princely stable, he did, where it was possible to see your reflection on the walls: beechwood cribs for every stall, brass rings, partition bars padded with leather and posts with shiny rounded tops.

Oh, well!

The young Prince, entirely devoted to those noisy carriages which create not only (bear with me!) a stink but also a trail of smoke at the rear, and which dash off on their own power, wasn't satisfied with having already three times run the risk of breaking his neck: just as soon as the old Princess (who, bless her, had never wanted to have anything to do with those devils) had been stricken with paralysis, he had lost no time in getting rid of him (Blackie) as well as Raven Black, the last two horses left in the stable, for his mother's tranquil landau.

Poor Raven Black, who knows where he had ended up, after so many years of honorable service!

Kind Giuseppe, the old coachman, had promised them that he would go and, together with the other old, trusted servants, kiss the hand of the Princess, who was now confined to an armchair for good, and would intercede for them.

But no! From the way in which the kind old man, who had returned quickly, had patted their necks and flanks, immediately both of them had understood that all hope was lost and their fate decided. They would be sold.

And indeed . . .

Blackie still failed to comprehend where he had gotten to. It wasn't bad, not really bad. Of course, it wasn't the Princess' stable. But this was a good stable, too. More than twenty horses, all black and on the old side, but with a good presence, dignified and full of gravity. Oh, as for gravity, they may even have had too much!

Blackie doubted whether even they understood properly the work to which they were assigned. On the contrary, it seemed to him that they were all constantly thinking about it, but without coming to any conclusion. That slow swaying of flowing tails, that scraping of hooves, from time to time, were unerring indicators of horses in deep reflection.

Only that Fofo was sure, perfectly sure, that he had fully understood everything.

Vulgar and presumptuous animal!

An old army horse, rejected after three years of service, because—to hear him tell it—some light-cavalry bumpkin from the Abruzzi had broken his wind, he did nothing but talk and talk and talk.

Blackie, with his heart still full of regret for his old friend Raven Black, couldn't stand Fofo. What jarred him most of all was that familiar behavior of his, and then his constant criticism of their stablemates.

God, what a tongue!

Not one of the twenty escaped! This one was like this, that one was like that . . .

"That tail . . . just look over there, if you please, and tell me whether that's a tail! If that's any way to move one's tail! Some energy, huh?

"That's a doctor's horse, I'm telling you.

"And over there, there, look at that fine Calabrian nag, how gracefully he wiggles his pig's ears . . . And what a fine forelock! And what a fine chin groove! He's another live wire, don't you think?

"Every once in a while he dreams he's not a gelding, and he wants to make love to that mare over there, three stalls to the right, see her?—with a face that looks so old, low in the forequarters, with her belly scraping the ground.

"But would you even call that a mare? That's a cow, let me tell you. And if you knew how she moves, as if in riding school! She looks as if her hooves were scalded whenever she touched the ground! . . . And yet, does she get foamed up! Sure, because she has a tender mouth. She has yet to grow her incisors to an even height, imagine that!"

It did Blackie no good to show that Fofo in every possible way that he was paying him no mind. Fofo would just rage on all the more.

To spite him.

"You know where we are? We're in a shipping agency. There are all kinds. This one is called the funeral type.

"You know what funeral means? It means pulling a black wagon with a peculiar shape—high, with four posts that support the canopy—and decorated all over with flounces and curtains and gilding: in short, a big, beautiful, luxury carriage; but it's all a waste, I assure you, all a waste, because you'll see that no one ever gets into it.

"There's only the coachman, looking as serious as he can, on his box.

"And they move slowly, always at a walking pace. Oh, there's no danger of your working up a sweat and getting a rubdown when you come back, or that the coachman will ever give you a lash or hurry you up in any other way!

"Slow—slow—slow.

"You always get where you need to get to in plenty of time.

"And that wagon—I understand it clearly—must be something held in special veneration by man.

"As I mentioned, no one dares to get inside; and, as soon as it's seen standing in front of a house, everybody stops and stares at it with long, frightened faces; many people even gather around it with lighted tapers; and then, as soon as we start to move, all of them accompany it from behind, in total silence.

"Often there's a band in front of us, too, a band, my friend, playing a kind of music that makes your guts drop out.

"Listen, you've got the bad habit of snorting and moving your head too much. Well, you've got to get rid of habits like that. If you snort for no reason, just imagine what will happen when you hear that music!

"Our work is easy, there's no denying; but it takes orderliness and solemnity. No snorting, no pitching. It's already too much when they allow you to shake your tail, just barely.

"Because the wagon that we're pulling, I'm telling you again, is highly respected. You'll find out that, on seeing us pass by, everybody lifts his hat.

"Do you know how I understood that it must be connected with shipping? I understood it from this.

"About two years ago, I was standing still, with one of our canopied wagons, in front of the big railing of the building that is our normal destination.

"You'll see that big railing! Behind it there are many dark, pointed trees that extend in two long, straight, endless lines, leaving some beautiful green lawns here and there with plenty of good, rich grass to eat; but that's all wasted, too: woe to you if you put out your lips toward it as you pass by.

"Enough of that. I was standing still there when a poor old comrade of mine from my days of army service came up beside me; he had really come down in the world: imagine, he was pulling an iron-fitted truck, one of those long, low, springless ones.

"He said:

"'Do you see me? Oh, Fofo, I'm really worn out!'

"'What line of work?' I asked him."

"And he:

"'Transporting boxes, all day long, from a shipping agency to the customs office.'

"'Boxes?' I said. 'What boxes?'

"'Heavy ones!' he said. 'Really heavy! Boxes full of goods to be shipped . . .'

"That was a relevation to me.

"Because you ought to know that we, too, transport a kind of very long box. They place it very slowly (everything always goes very slowly) into our wagon, from the back; and while that procedure is going on, the people all around take off their hats and just stare in an awed way. Who knows why? But surely, if we, too, deal in boxes, it must be connected with shipping, don't you think so?

"What the devil does that box contain? It's heavy, just you believe me! Lucky that we always transport one at a time . . .

"Merchandise to be shipped, certainly. But what kind of merchandise, if—as soon as it comes into view—every passerby gives so many indications of respect, and the shipping is done with so much pomp and ceremony?

"At a given moment, usually (not always), we stop in front of a majestic building that may be the customs office for our shipments. From the doorway there step forward certain men decked out in a black underskirt, with their shirt worn outside (I suppose they're the customs officers); the box is taken out of the wagon; everybody takes his hat off again; and those men mark the box with an official permit.

"Where all those precious goods that we ship go to—that, you see, I haven't yet managed to understand. But I have some suspicion that not even the humans understand it perfectly, and I console myself.

"To tell the truth, the magnificence of the boxes and the solemnity of the proceedings could lead you to believe that the humans must know *something* about these shipments of theirs. But they look too uncertain and awed to me. And from the long acquaintance I now have with them, I have derived this much experience: humans do many, many things, my friend, without knowing at all why they do them!"

As Fofo had deduced that morning from the head groom's curses: saddlecloths, tassels and plumes. Four horses to draw the carriage. It was really a first-class job.

"Did you see?"

Blackie found himself harnessed between the shafts with Fofo. And Fofo, naturally, continued to bore him with his eternal explanations.

But he, too, was bothered that morning by the imposition put on him by the head groom, who, when there were four horses, always harnessed him between the shafts and never to the splinter bar for extra horses.[1]

"What a dog! Because, you realize, these two here in front of us are just for show. What do they pull? They don't pull a damn thing! We're the ones who pull. And we go so slowly! Now they're taking a nice little walk to stretch their legs, all decked out in gala . . . And just look at what sort of animals I'm forced to see get the preference over myself! Recognize them?"

They were the two black horses that Fofo had dubbed "doctor's horse" and "Calabrian nag."

"That damned Calabrian . . . You have him in front of *you*, lucky you! You'll smell him, my friend; you'll become aware that his ears aren't the only piglike thing about him, and you'll thank the head groom, who protects him and gives him double rations of fodder . . . It takes luck in this world—don't snort. Are you starting already? Keep your head still! Whew, if you act like that today, my friend, you'll get so many tugs on the reins that you'll have a bloody mouth, I'm telling you. There will be speeches today. You'll see how jolly it is! One speech, two speeches, three speeches . . . I've

---

[1] Using different terms, Fofo and Blackie are "wheelers" and the other two horses are "leaders."

even come across a first-class funeral with five speeches! Enough
to make you crazy . . . Three hours of standing still, with all these
decorations on you that don't allow you to breathe: your legs
cramped, your tail imprisoned, your ears between two
holes . . . Jolly, with the flies biting you under your tail! What are
the speeches? Who knows? I really don't understand, to tell the
truth . . . These first-class shipments must be very complicated
ones. And maybe, in those speeches, they're giving the instructions.
One isn't enough, and they make two; two aren't enough, and they
make three. They sometimes make as many as five, as I said: there
I was, my friend, with an urge to kick out right and left, and then
start rolling on the ground like a madcap . . . Maybe it will be the
same today. Full gala! Did you see the coachmen, how he's tricked
out, too? And there are also the ushers, the taper-bearers . . . Tell
me, are you skittish?"

"I don't understand . . . "

"You know: do you shy easily? Because, you'll see, in a little while
they'll put the lighted tapers right under your nose . . . Easy,
there . . . easy! What's got into you? You see? The first tug on the
reins . . . Did it hurt you? Well, you'll get a lot of them today, let
me tell you . . . But what are you doing? Are you crazy? Don't
stretch out your neck like that! (Nice baby, are you swimming?[2]
Are you playing a kicking game?)[3] "Stay still . . . Oh, really? Take
that tug, and that! Hey! Watch out, now you're making them tug
at my mouth, too! Say, this one is crazy! My God, my God, this one
is really crazy! He's panting, he's neighing, he's whinnying, he's
turning in a circle; what's going on? Look at him prancing! He's
crazy, he's crazy! Going into a prance while he's pulling a first-class
wagon!"

Blackie did indeed seem to have lost his mind; he was panting,
neighing, pawing the ground and trembling all over. The lackeys
had to leap down from the carriage in hot haste to hold him still
in front of the doorway of the manor house where they were to
stop, amid a large throng of stiff gentlemen in frockcoats and top
hats.

"What's going on?" was the cry everywhere. "Oh, look, a horse
of the funeral carriage is rearing up!"

And all the people, in great confusion, surrounded the carriage,
curious, dismayed, surprised, shocked. The ushers had not yet

managed to hold Blackie still. The coachman had risen to his feet and was pulling the reins furiously. In vain. Blackie kept on lashing out with his hooves and neighing; he was foaming, with his head turned toward the doorway of the house.

He only calmed down when there came out of that door and arrived on the scene an old servant in livery, who, shoving aside the ushers, took him by the bridle and immediately, on recognizing him, started to exclaim with tears in his eyes:

"Why, it's Blackie! It's Blackie! Oh, poor Blackie . . . Why, of course he acts this way . . . The mistress' horse! The late Princess' horse! He recognized the house . . . he smells the odor of his own stable . . . Poor Blackie, poor Blackie . . . behave, behave . . . yes, you see? It's me, your old Giuseppe . . . Behave, yes . . . Poor Blackie, it's up to you to carry her—see?—your mistress . . . It's up to you, poor thing, you who still remember . . . She'll be pleased to be conveyed by you for the last time . . . "

Then he turned to the coachman, who, infuriated by the bad showing that the funeral establishment was making in front of all those gentlemen, was continuing to tug violently on the reins and threatening to whip the horse, and shouted at him:

"Enough! Stop! I've got him under control here . . . He's gentle as a lamb . . . Sit back down. I'll guide him the whole way . . . We'll go together—right, Blackie?—to leave our kind mistress . . . Slowly and quietly, as usual, right? And you'll behave, so you don't hurt her, poor old Blackie, you who still remember . . . They've already enclosed her in the box; now they're carrying her down . . . "

At this moment Fofo, who was listening to all this from the other side of the shafts, asked in amazement:

"It's your mistress inside the box?"

Blackie gave him a sidelong kick.

But Fofo was too absorbed by this new revelation to be offended.

"Ah, so we . . . ," he kept on saying to himself, "ah, so we . . . what about that! . . . it's what *I* meant to say . . . This old man is crying; I've seen so many others crying, other times . . . and so many awed faces . . . and that depressing music . . . Now I understand it all, I understand it all . . . *That's* why our work is so easy! It's only when humans cry that *we* can be cheerful and relaxed . . . "

And he too felt the temptation to prance.

MRS. FROLA AND MR. PONZA, HER SON-IN-LAW

But after all, can you imagine? Everybody may really go mad because they can't decide which of the two is the crazy one, that Mrs. Frola or that Mr. Ponza, her son-in-law. Things like this only happen in Valdana, an unlucky town that attracts every kind of eccentric outsider!

She is crazy or *he* is crazy; there's no middle ground: one of the two *must* be crazy. Because what's involved is nothing less than this . . . No, it's better to start off explaining things in their proper order.

I assure you, I'm seriously alarmed by the anxiety in which the inhabitants of Valdana have been living for three months, and I'm not much concerned for Mrs. Frola and Mr. Ponza, her son-in-law. Because, even if it's true that a grave misfortune has befallen them, it's no less true that one of them, at least, has had the good luck to be driven crazy by it and the other one has aided and is continuing to aid the victim, in such a way that, I repeat, no one can manage to know for sure which of the two is really crazy; and, certainly, they couldn't have comforted each other in a better way than that. But I ask you, do you think it's nothing to keep the entire citizenry under such a nightmarish burden, knocking out all the props of their reasoning capacity so that they can no longer distinguish between illusion and reality? It's anguish, perpetual dismay. Everyone sees those two daily, looks at their faces, knows that one of the two is crazy, studies them, scrutinizes them, spies on them and—no use! Impossible to discover which of the two it is; where illusion lies, where reality lies. Naturally, there arises in each mind the pernicious suspicion that, in that case, reality counts for no more than illusion does, and that every reality may very well be an illusion, and vice versa. You think it's nothing? If I were in the governor's[1] shoes, for the mental well-being of the inhabitants of Valdana I

---

[1] *Prefetto*, chief officer of a *provincia* (Italy is divided into "provinces" administratively).

wouldn't hesitate to give Mrs. Frola and Mr. Ponza, her son-in-law, their walking papers.

But let's proceed in an orderly fashion.

This Mr. Ponza arrived in Valdana three months ago as a secretary in the governor's office. He took lodgings in the new apartment house at the edge of town, the one called "the Honeycomb." There. On the top floor, a tiny flat. Three windows looking out at the countryside, high, sad windows (because the housefront on that side, exposed to the north wind, facing all those pallid market gardens, although it's new, has become so deteriorated, who knows why?), and three inner windows, on this side, facing the courtyard, which is encircled by the railing of the top gallery, divided into sections by grated partitions. Hanging from that railing, all the way up, are a large number of little baskets ready to be lowered on ropes as needed.

At the same time, however, to everyone's amazement, Mr. Ponza rented another small furnished flat, three rooms and kitchen, in the center of town, Number 15 Via dei Santi, to be exact. He said it was to be used by his mother-in-law, Mrs. Frola. And she did indeed arrive five or six days later; and Mr. Ponza, all alone, went to meet her at the station, took her to the apartment and left her there by herself.

Now, please! You can understand it if a daughter, on getting married, leaves her mother's house to go and live with her husband, even in another town; but when that mother, not bearing to remain far from her daughter, leaves her hometown, her own house, and follows her, and when, in the town where both she and her daughter are strangers, she goes to live in a separate house, *that* is no longer so easily understood; or else one must assume such a strong incompatibility between mother-in-law and son-in-law that their all living together is impossible, even under these circumstances.

Naturally, that's what people in Valdana thought at first. And certainly the one who came off the worst in everyone's opinion because of this was Mr. Ponza. When it came to Mrs. Frola, if someone granted that she might perhaps be partly to blame in this, either through a lack of indulgence or through some obstinacy or intolerance, everybody was favorably impressed by the maternal love that drew her close to her daughter, even though condemned not to be able to live by her side.

A great part was played in this favoring of Mrs. Frola and in the image of Mr. Ponza that was immediately stamped on everyone's

mind—namely, that he was a hard, no! a cruel man—by their physical appearance as well, it must be said. Thickset, neckless, dark as
an African, with thick, coarse hair hanging over his low forehead,
dense, bristly eyebrows that meet over his nose, a big shiny mustache like a policeman's, and in his eyes—melancholy, staring, almost without any white—a violent, exasperated, barely restrained
intensity—whether from sad pain or from irritation at other people's glances, it was hard to say—Mr. Ponza is certainly one whose
looks don't make him readily liked or trusted. On the other hand,
Mrs. Frola is a frail, pale little old lady, with elegant, very noble
features and an air of melancholy, but a weightless, vague and sweet
melancholy that doesn't keep her from being affable to everyone.

Now, as soon as she came to town, Mrs. Frola exhibited this affa-
bility, so natural in her, and, because of that, the aversion for Mr.
Ponza immediately increased in everybody's mind; because everyone clearly perceived her character—as not only gentle, humble,
tolerant, but also full of indulgent understanding for the wrong
that her son-in-law is doing her; and also because it came to be
known that Mr. Ponza is not satisfied to relegate that poor mother
to a separate house, but also pushes his cruelty to the point of
forbidding her to see her daughter.

Except that, on her visits to the ladies of Valdana, Mrs. Frola
immediately protests: "Not cruelty, not cruelty," thrusting out her
little hands, sincerely distressed that people can think such a thing
about her son-in-law. And she hurriedly praises all his virtues, saying all the good about him that's possible and imaginable: how
much love, how much care, how many attentions he lavishes not
only on her daughter but also on her, yes, yes, also on her; solicitous,
selfless . . . Oh, not cruel, no, for heaven's sake! There's only this:
that Mr. Ponza wants to have his wife entirely to himself, to such
an extent that he wants even the love she must have for her mother
(and he admits it, of course) to reach her not directly but through
him, as intermediary, that's it! Yes, this may look like cruelty, but
it's not; it's something else, something that she, Mrs. Frola, understands perfectly and is anguished at being unable to express. His
nature, that's what . . . but no, perhaps a kind of illness . . . how to
put it? My goodness, you just have to look at his eyes. At first those
eyes may make a bad impression; but they say it all to anyone who
can read them as she can: they speak of the sealed-up fullness of
a whole world of love within him, in which his wife must live without
ever leaving it for a moment, and into which no one else, not even

her mother, must enter. Jealousy? Yes, perhaps; but only if you want to give a cheap name to this exclusive totality of love. Selfishness? If so, it's a selfishness that makes him give all of himself, like a world, to his own lady! When you get to the bottom of it, you might call it selfishness in *her* that she desires to break open this closed world of love, to make her way into it by force, when she knows that her daughter is happy and so adored . . . That should be enough for a mother! Besides, it's not at all true that she doesn't see her daughter. She sees her two or three times a day: she goes into the courtyard of the building; she rings the bell and immediately her daughter comes to the window up there.

"How are you, Tildina?"

"Fine, Mother. And you?"

"As God wishes, daughter. Send down the basket!"

And in the basket there's always a short note with the events of the day. There! that's enough for her. This life has been going on for four years now, and Mrs. Frola has already gotten used to it. Yes, she's resigned to it. And she practically no longer suffers from it.

As you can easily understand, this resigned attitude of Mrs. Frola's, her saying that she has gotten used to her torment, redounds all the more to the discredit of Mr. Ponza, her son-in-law, the more that she strains herself to excuse him in that long speech of hers.

Therefore it is with real indignation and, I may add, even with fear, that the ladies of Valdana to whom Mrs. Frola paid her first visit receive the notice on the following day of another unexpected visit, from Mr. Ponza, who begs them to grant him just two minutes of audience, for a "dutiful declaration," if it's not inconvenient.

Red in the face, almost as if he were having a stroke, with his eyes harder and sadder than ever, in his hand a handkerchief whose whiteness, like that of his cuffs and shirt collar, clashes with the darkness of his skin, body hair and suit, Mr. Ponza, continually wiping away the perspiration dripping from his low forehead and stubbly, purplish cheeks—not from the heat, but from the very evident violence of the control he is exerting over himself, which also causes a trembling in his large hands with their long nails—in this parlor and in that, in front of those ladies staring at him as if in fright, first asks whether Mrs. Frola, his mother-in-law, came to visit them the day before; then, with his sorrow, effort and agitation constantly increasing, asks whether she spoke to them about her daughter and told them that he absolutely forbids her to see her and go up to his apartment.

The ladies, seeing him so upset, as you may easily imagine, quickly reply that it's true, yes, Mrs. Frola did tell them about being forbidden to see her daughter, but also said all the good about him that's possible and imaginable, to the extent of not only excusing him, but also not giving him a shred of blame for that very prohibition.

Except that, instead of calming down at this reply from the ladies, Mr. Ponza gets even more upset; his eyes become harder, more staring, sadder; the big drops of sweat fall more heavily; and finally, making an even more violent effort at self-control, he comes to his "dutiful declaration."

Which is simply this: that Mrs. Frola, poor woman, doesn't look it, but she's crazy.

Yes, she's been crazy for four years. And her madness takes this very form: her belief that he refuses to allow her to see her daughter. What daughter? She's dead, her daughter died four years ago; and it was precisely from her grief at that death that Mrs. Frola went mad; yes, and it's a good thing she went mad, because for her, madness was the release from her desperate sorrow. Naturally she could only escape it in this manner; namely, by believing that it wasn't true her daughter had died, and that instead it's he, her son-in-law, who won't let her see her any more.

Purely out of a duty of charity toward an unhappy creature, he, Mr. Ponza, has for four years, at the cost of many serious sacrifices, been humoring that pathetic delusion: at an expense beyond his means, he maintains two households, one for him and one for her; and he makes his second wife, who by good luck is charitably willing to go along, humor that delusion, too. But charity, duty—look, they can go only so far: in his capacity as a civil servant as well, Mr. Ponza can't permit the people in town to think such a cruel and improbable thing about him; namely, that out of jealousy or any other reason, he forbids a poor mother to see her own daughter.

After this declaration, Mr. Ponza makes a bow to those bewildered ladies, and leaves. But this bewilderment of the ladies doesn't even have the time to diminish a little, when there appears Mrs. Frola again with her gentle air of vague melancholy, asking forgiveness if, on her account, the kind ladies were somewhat frightened by the visit of Mr. Ponza, her son-in-law.

And Mrs. Frola, with the greatest simplicity and naturalness in the world, declares in her turn, but in strict confidence, for heaven's sake! because Mr. Ponza is a civil servant and for that very reason she refrained from saying this the first time, yes, because this could seriously damage his career; Mr. Ponza, poor man—an excellent, excellent irreproachable secretary at the governor's office, perfect, precise in all his actions, in all his thoughts, full of so many good qualities—Mr. Ponza, poor man, in this matter alone is no longer . . . no longer in his right mind; there you have it; the crazy one is he, poor man; and his madness takes this very form: his belief that his wife died four years ago and his going around saying that the crazy one is she, Mrs. Frola, who believes her daughter is still alive. No, he isn't doing this in order somehow to justify to others that almost maniacal jealousy of his and that cruelty of forbidding her to see her daughter; no, the poor man believes, seriously believes that his wife is dead and the one he has with him is a second wife. A most pitiful case! Because, to tell the truth, with his excessive love this man at first ran the risk of destroying, of killing his young, fragile little wife, so much so that it was necessary to get her out of his hands secretly and put her into a nursing home without his knowledge. Well, the poor man, whose mind had already been seriously weakened by this frenzied love, went mad from this; he thought his wife had really died: and this idea became so fixed in his mind that there was no longer any way to remove it, not even when his wife, back home after about a year, and as healthy as before, was brought before him. He thought she was a different woman; so that, with the aid of everybody, relatives and friends, it was necessary to simulate a second wedding, which fully restored the balance of his mental faculties.

Now, Mrs. Frola believes she has some right to suspect that for some time her son-in-law has been completely himself again and that he is pretending, only pretending to believe that his wife is a second wife, in order to keep her entirely to himself, without contact with anyone, because perhaps from time to time he nevertheless is smitten with the fear that she may be secretly taken away from him again.

Yes! Otherwise, how could you explain all the care, all the solicitude, he has for her, his mother-in-law, if he really believes that the woman he has with him is a second wife? He ought not to feel the obligation of so much consideration for a woman who in fact would no longer be his mother-in-law, right? Note that Mrs. Frola says this, not to give an even better proof that *he* is the crazy one; but to prove even to herself that her suspicion is well founded.

"And meanwhile," she concludes with a sigh that on her lips assumes the form of a sweet, very sad smile, "meanwhile my poor daughter has to pretend she's not herself but someone else; and I am also obliged to pretend I'm crazy to believe my daughter is still alive. It doesn't cost me much, thank God, because my daughter is there, well and full of life; I see her, I speak to her; but I'm condemned not to be able to live with her, and also to see her and speak to her only from a distance, so that he can keep on believing, or pretending to believe, that my daughter, God forbid, is dead and the woman he has with him is a second wife. But I say once more, what's the difference if, on these terms, we have succeeded in restoring peace of mind to both of them? I know that my daughter is adored, contented; I see her; I speak to her; and I resign myself, out of love for her and for him; to live this way and even to be considered a madwoman, madam—patience! . . ."

I ask you, don't you think that things are at such a pass in Valdana that we all go around with open mouths, looking each other in the eye, like lunatics? Who of the two is to be believed? Who is the crazy one? Where is the reality, where the illusion?

Mr. Ponza's wife would be able to tell us. But there's no trusting her when, in his presence, she says she is the second wife; just as there's no trusting her when, in Mrs. Frola's presence, she confirms the statement that she's her daughter. It would be necessary to take her aside and make her tell the truth privately. But that's impossible. Mr. Ponza—whether or not he's the crazy one—is really very jealous and doesn't let anybody see his wife. He keeps her up there, as if in prison, under lock and key; and without a doubt this fact is in Mrs. Frola's favor; but Mr. Ponza says he is compelled to do this, in fact that his wife herself makes him do it, for fear that Mrs. Frola will unexpectedly come into the house. That may be an excuse. But it's also a fact that Mr. Ponza doesn't even have one maid in the house. He says he does it to save money, obliged as he is to pay rent on two apartments; and in the meantime he himself assumes the burden of doing the daily marketing; and his wife, who according to her own statements is not Mrs. Frola's daughter, out of pity for her—that is, for a poor old woman who was formerly her husband's mother-in-law—also takes it upon herself to attend to all the household chores, even the most humble, doing without the aid of a servant. It seems a bit much to everybody. But it's also true that if this state of affairs can't be explained by pity, it can be explained by his jealousy.

Meanwhile, the governor of Valdana has been satisfied with Mr. Ponza's declaration. But surely the latter's appearance and in large part his conduct do not speak in his favor, at least for the ladies of Valdana, who are all more inclined to give credence to Mrs. Frola. Indeed, that lady comes solicitously to show them the loving notes that her daughter sends down to her in the little basket, as well as many other private documents, the credibility of which, however, is totally denied by Mr. Ponza, who says that they were delivered to her to bolster the pious deception.

One thing is certain anyway: that both of them manifest a marvelous, deeply moving spirit of sacrifice for each other; and that each of them has the most exquisitely compassionate consideration for the presumed madness of the other. Both of them state their case with wonderful rationality; so that it would never have occurred to anyone in Valdana to say that either of them was crazy, if they hadn't said it themselves: Mr. Ponza about Mrs. Frola, and Mrs. Frola about Mr. Ponza.

Mrs. Frola often goes to see her son-in-law at the governor's office to get some advice from him, or waits for him when he comes out so he can accompany her to do some shopping; and very often, for his part, in his free time and every evening Mr. Ponza goes to visit Mrs. Frola in her little furnished flat; and every time they accidentally run into each other in the street they immediately continue on together with the greatest cordiality; he lets her walk on the right and, if she's tired, he offers his arm, and so they go off together, amid the sullen anger, amazement and dismay of the people who study them, scrutinize them, spy on them, but—no use!—cannot yet in any way manage to understand which of the two is the crazy one, where the illusion is, where the reality.

DOVER · THRIFT · EDITIONS

All books complete and unabridged. All 5³⁄₁₆″ × 8¼″, paperbound.
Just $1.00–$2.00 in U.S.A.

A selection of the more than 100 titles in the series:

FLATLAND: A ROMANCE OF MANY DIMENSIONS, Edwin A. Abbott. 96pp. 27263-X $1.00

DOVER BEACH AND OTHER POEMS, Matthew Arnold. 112pp. 28037-3 $1.00

CIVIL WAR STORIES, Ambrose Bierce. 128pp. 28038-1 $1.00

THE DEVIL'S DICTIONARY, Ambrose Bierce. 144pp. 27542-6 $1.00

SONGS OF INNOCENCE AND SONGS OF EXPERIENCE, William Blake. 64pp. 27051-3 $1.00

SONNETS FROM THE PORTUGUESE AND OTHER POEMS, Elizabeth Barrett Browning. 64pp. 27052-1 $1.00

MY LAST DUCHESS AND OTHER POEMS, Robert Browning. 128pp. 27783-6 $1.00

SELECTED POEMS, George Gordon, Lord Byron. 112pp. 27784-4 $1.00

ALICE'S ADVENTURES IN WONDERLAND, Lewis Carroll. 96pp. 27543-4 $1.00

O PIONEERS!, Willa Cather. 128pp. 27785-2 $1.00

THE CHERRY ORCHARD, Anton Chekhov. 64pp. 26682-6 $1.00

THE AWAKENING, Kate Chopin. 128pp. 27786-0 $1.00

THE RIME OF THE ANCIENT MARINER AND OTHER POEMS, Samuel Taylor Coleridge. 80pp. 27266-4 $1.00

HEART OF DARKNESS, Joseph Conrad. 80pp. 26464-5 $1.00

THE RED BADGE OF COURAGE, Stephen Crane. 112pp. 26465-3 $1.00

A CHRISTMAS CAROL, Charles Dickens. 80pp. 26865-9 $1.00

THE CRICKET ON THE HEARTH AND OTHER CHRISTMAS STORIES, Charles Dickens. 128pp. 28039-X $1.00

SELECTED POEMS, Emily Dickinson. 64pp. 26466-1 $1.00

SELECTED POEMS, John Donne. 96pp. 27788-7 $1.00

NOTES FROM THE UNDERGROUND, Fyodor Dostoyevsky. 96pp. 27053-X $1.00

SIX GREAT SHERLOCK HOLMES STORIES, Sir Arthur Conan Doyle. 112pp. 27055-6 $1.00

THE SOULS OF BLACK FOLK, W. E. B. Du Bois. 176pp. 28041-1 $2.00

MEDEA, Euripides. 64pp. 27548-5 $1.00

A BOY'S WILL AND NORTH OF BOSTON, Robert Frost. 112pp. (Available in U.S. only) 26866-7 $1.00

WHERE ANGELS FEAR TO TREAD, E. M. Forster. 128pp. (Available in U.S. only) 27791-7 $1.00

FAUST, PART ONE, Johann Wolfgang von Goethe. 192pp. 28046-2 $2.00

THE SCARLET LETTER, Nathaniel Hawthorne. 192pp. 28048-9 $2.00

A DOLL'S HOUSE, Henrik Ibsen. 80pp. 27062-9 $1.00

THE TURN OF THE SCREW, Henry James. 96pp. 26684-2 $1.00

VOLPONE, Ben Jonson. 112pp. 28049-7 $1.00

DUBLINERS, James Joyce. 160pp. 26870-5 $1.00

A PORTRAIT OF THE ARTIST AS A YOUNG MAN, James Joyce. 192pp. 28050-0 $2.00

LYRIC POEMS, John Keats. 80pp. 26871-3 $1.00

THE BOOK OF PSALMS, King James Bible. 144pp. 27541-8 $1.00